BY THE RIVERS
OF MAZOVIA

BY THE RIVERS
OF **MAZOVIA**

Mikhoel Burshtin

TRANSLATED FROM THE YIDDISH BY
Jordan Finkin

Naydus Press
Cincinnati, Ohio
2023

Published 2023 by Naydus Press
Printed in the Unites States of America
Cover design by Lindsay Lake
Cover illustration by Issachar Ryback

First Edition

Naydus Press is a non-profit, 401(c)(3) organization dedicated to increasing awareness of and access to Yiddish literature by supporting Yiddish translators and publishing their translation into English. Our goal is to bring the best of Yiddish literature to new generations of readers.

ISBN 978-1-7341936-3-3

To Margalit (Małgorzata) Tal
with deep friendship and gratitude

CONTENTS

ACKNOWLEDGEMENTS

Naydus Press wishes to express its gratitude to the following for their financial support:

The Hornik Family Foundation

INTRODUCTION

The pages of this book resound with the song: "We shall not hang our harps upon the willows above the rivers of Mazovia, nor shall our song fall silent."—Naftoli Vaynig (from a review of the novel)

This epigraph offers an apt summary of the animating spirit of the book. Just as Jews have succeeded in the most vibrant transformation of exile into diaspora, so too does Mikhoel Burshtin transmute the somber Psalm's rejection of the ability to sing into an injunction to create and build, even in the face of scorn, abuse, or worse. *By the Rivers of Mazovia*, part of the last efflorescence of Polish Yiddish literature before the Second World War, gives us a painterly glimpse into the lives of a Polish shtetl's cast of characters as they navigate a rapidly changing and often precarious existence.

Mikhoel Burshtin (Michal Bursztyn) (1897–1945) was born west of Warsaw in the town of Bloyne (Błonie in Polish). At the age of thirteen he ran away from home and for two years worked as a laborer, including at a lumberyard. He read widely during those years, and at fifteen he moved to Warsaw to attend high school. After earning a teaching certification in literature and history, he worked as a schoolteacher until the Second World War. Throughout his writing career he published novels and short stories that were largely well received. He was at work on another novel while in the Kovno ghetto before being sent to his death in Dachau.

Burshtin has been described as a journalistic writer, alert to the details of current events, which become woven into the loose patterns of his narratives. He manages these fragmentary associations to make keen but subtle observations on the perils of Jewish life, from family struggles and economic tensions, to political turmoil and anti-Semitism. Burshtin, one critic noted, was "more a painter than a narrator." Apart from his collection of short stories, *Broyt un zalts* (Bread and Salt; 1939), his major novels comprise a loose trilogy of Polish-Jewish life from the mid-1910s to the mid-1930s. These novels—*Iber di khurves fun Ployne* (Over the Ruins of Ployne; 1931), *Goyrl* (Fate; 1936), and *Bay di taykhn fun Mazovye* (By the Rivers of Mazovia; 1937)—are realist explorations of the Polish shtetl as their Jews navigate the challenges of modernity.

The region of central Poland from which this novel takes its name is watered by two major rivers, the Vistula and the Bug. The title, echoing Psalm 137, implies a parallel between this home for both Poles and Jews and that other fraught mesopotamian land of diaspora. However, while there are mournful resonances between that poem and the present novel, the latter is not ultimately an elegiac work. True, what the peoples share in land and in life they do not share in suffering—a point brought home at key points in the novel—yet the great leveling force of death ultimately has more purchase on their common history than enmity.

At is simplest, the novel tells the story of the Jews of the fictional Mazovian town of Smolin from around 1935 to 1936. (The narrative mentions the death of the Polish leader Józef Piłsudski, which occurred in May of 1935; and the pogrom featured at the book's end echoes the pogrom in the Mazovian town of Przytyk in March of 1936.) The narrative revolves around two axes: Hersh Lustik, the honest, jovial orchard keeper who acts as the de facto leader and beating heart of the Jewish community, somewhat in the vein of Tevye the dairyman; and Gabriel Priver, the local intellectual who, having gone to the big city to become a doctor, now finds himself back in his hometown to hang out his shingle after failed attempts elsewhere. The shtetl study in contrast between the simple salt of the earth and the deracinated intellectual shows clear signs of overuse in Yiddish literature. *By the Rivers of Mazovia* is no exception. Yet while a timeworn topos might strain the patience of the jaded reader, the other thematic tensions explored in the book within that framework amply compensate—namely, both the individual's and the community's connection to *place*. Briefly put, the novel offers a deep examination of the complications of nativeness. And in particular, it scrutinizes anti-Semitism as one element of the Jews' relationship with their place in Poland.

Consider, for example, how the book ends in the same place in which it began—the cemetery. Occupying a central position in Yiddish literature, the cemetery has long offered Yiddish writers an ironic opening to consideration of both Jews' physical presence in a location and their figurative participation in its history. Sholem Aleichem, for example, often reads the cemetery as an historical document, a lapidary local chronicle of Jewish life. That is no less Burshtin's goal—a roughly one-year chronicle of Jewish Smolin bookended by the cemetery.

The cemetery of the first scene is where the soldiers who fought in the First World War are buried. Though the war has been over but some seventeen years, the wounds of the cataclysm are still fresh. As if to foreground the humanistic message at the heart of the novel, Burshtin paints the cemetery as the great cosmopolitan ideal, where Jews and Christians, peasants and bourgeois, Ukrainians, Belarusians, Prussians, Poles, and Jews—religions, classes, and nationalities—intermingle harmoniously.

To emphasize the organic nature of these communities' "collaboration," Burshtin opens with a remarkable image of dismemberment, no less striking than the dog carrying the severed hand at the beginning of *Yojimbo*. Burshtin describes how every year the autumn winds unearth desiccated human bones, which farmers collect and grind for meal to fertilize their fields. For all its grimness, could there be a more powerful metaphor for indigeneity? And with the tragic interments at the novel's conclusion, Burshtin underscores the guardedly hopeful message on which he ends.

Complicating that connection to place, and playing with the grim and ominous undertones of death, stands anti-Semitism. The bulk of the novel is taken up with the struggles of daily life among the Jews of Smolin, their family squabbles and personal frailties. All of this, however, is acted out under the ever-present shadow of anti-Semitism. It is the simmering anxiety that bubbles over and stains every relationship in the book.

Burshtin presents a typology of three kinds of anti-Semitism. The first, a more-or-less mild form, is summed up in the person of the mayor. A friend of Hersh's since their youth, his sympathy for the Jews is tempered by the occasional off-hand pejorative comment, which Hersh seems to shrug off in the name of their friendship. It is the mayor more than anyone else in the novel who is interested in Zionism as a cure for the Jews' ills. Even here, however, Hersh remains cautious. As he notes midway through the novel: "Nowadays you have to be careful. There's a hair's breadth between loving Jews and hating them."

The second type is what we might call a rather routine form, embodied by the German colonist farmer Witbrot and the Polish forester. It is an acid tolerance, a balance between moments of overt hostility and grudging dismissal. Hersh offers a straightforward way of dealing with this type of anti-Semitism—the pleasure of Jewish irony. At one point, when the Jews are freezing in the cold winter, Hersh goes to the forester to get firewood. The forester responds with typical curses and a reluctance to help. Ultimately, Hersh prevails and on parting utters a traditional pious reply in Polish: *"Bóg zapłać!*—May God repay you well!" What is being repaid is left to the reader of course, but Hersh is not one known for turning the other cheek.

The third type is the malign form, which features in the climactic pogrom at the end of the book. In the catalogue of pogrom scenes in Yiddish literature, this one is distinct and unusual. To portray the events surrounding the disaster, Burshtin transports Smolin to China—and transposes it to Sama-lin—where Jew hatred is the province of the local "coolies," as they are called, and the pogrom itself is described as a massive impersonal storm, a typhoon which devastates the homes of the Jews. This striking reconfiguration has been credited to an attempt to placate the Polish censors. (Incidentally, the book has an interesting history with its censors. The first edition appeared in Warsaw in 1937. A Soviet edition came out in 1941, but it was edited so as not to run afoul of the censor during the period of the Molotov-Ribbentrop Pact, which shunned criticism of Germans and Germany. All mentions of Hitler, for example, were expurgated. The later edition published in Poland in 1951 followed the Soviet edition.) While this truckling to censorship is possible, the dramatic dislocation in this technique serves an additional purpose: it widens the breach between peoples, momentarily belying the myth of indigeneity, and allowing the pogrom to progress as a massive, inevitable, and inexorable force of nature.

At the end of the novel, the Jews process to the cemetery to bury their misfortunate dead. Hersh takes the opportunity, with the *kaddish* prayer echoing in the crowd's ears, to put his faith and his muscle into the rebuilding of their community. Hersh is clear about the message of the novel: Jewish indigenous habitation and creative participation in Poland is definitive, a fact to be affirmed and fought for, even against the headwinds of history.

Bibliography

Burshtin, Mikhoel, *Bay di taykhn fun Mazovye* (Warsaw: P.E.N. klub, 1937)

Shloyme Lastik, *Mitn ponim tsum morgn* (Warsaw: Yidish Bukh, 1952)

Leksikon fun der nayer Yidisher literatur, vol.1 (New York: Alveltlekher Yidisher Kultur-Kongres, 1956): cols. 273–275.

Avraham Novershtern, "Burshtin, Mikhoel" in: Gershon David Hundert, ed. *The YIVO Encyclopedia of Jews in Eastern Europe* (New Have: Yale University Press, 2008): 280–281.

Chone Shmeruk, "Responses to Antisemitism in Poland, 1912–36: A Case Study of the Novels of Michal Bursztyn" in: Juhuda Reinharz, ed. *Living with Antisemitism: Modern Jewish Responses* (Hanover: University Press of New England, 1987): 275–295.

Y. Y. Trunk, *Di Yidishe proze in Poyln in der tkufe tsvishn beyde velt-milkhomes* (Buenos Aires: Tsentral-Farband fun Poylishe Yidn in Argentine, 1949)

Naftoli Vaynig, "Bay di taykhn fun Mazovye: vegn M. Burshtins nay bukh" *Literarishe bleter* 15:19 (1938): 325–327.

Yoysef Volf, *Kritishe minyaturn* (Warsaw: [s.n.], 1940)

NOTE ON THE ILLUSTRATIONS

The cover illustration is "Di shul" ("The Old Synagogue") by the artist Issachar Ryback from his book *Mayn khorever heym* published in Berlin in 1922/1923 by Shveln.

The illustration for Part I was made by Todros Geller for the poetry collection *Kareln* by Pessi Hershfeld, published in Chicago in 1926 by L. M. Stein.

The illustration for Part II was made by A. Abramovits for the short story collection *Modne menshen* by Rokhl Luria, published in New York in 1918.

CAST OF CHARACTERS

Hersh Lustik: orchard keeper

Ratse ("Woebegone"): Hersh's wife

Soreh-Gitl: Ratse's sister; Volf's wife; Tsvetl's mother; Yisrultshe Blimeles and Zisl's elderly neighbor

Moshke: revolutionary; Soreh-Gitl's son; Tsvetl's brother

Tsvetl: knitter; Volf's daughter; Bertshik Shmatte's lover and Harshl's wife

Pesele: Tsvetl and Moshke's sister

Gabriel Priver: doctor

Shmuel Loyvitsher: dry-goods merchant; head of the Jewish community of Smolin

Sheva Loyvitsher: Shmuel Loyvitsher's wife; Khashe's sister; manages the dry-goods store; also Gabriel Priver's cousin

Golde Loyvitsher: Shmuel Loyvitsher's daughter; granddaughter of Yisrultshe Blimeles; and first cousin, once removed, of Gabriel Priver

Yisrultshe Blimeles: Sheva Loyvitsher and Khashe's father; Gabriel Priver's uncle

Zisl: Yisrultshe Blimeles's wife

Grunem ("the Long Suffering"): owner of a hand mill; Yisrultshe Blimeles's son-in-law

Khashe: Grunem's wife; Sheva's sister; Gabriel's cousin

Shloymele: Grunem and Khashe's son

Zlatke: Grunem and Khashe's daughter

Hadassah: Grunem and Khashe's daughter

Lazar Kurnik: poultryman

Fradl: Lazar Kurnik's wife

Bertshik Shmatte: peddler, then coachman

Yitte: healer and midwife; Bertshik's mother

Harshl: a bootmaker

Avreml "Treyf": butcher

Rabbi

Baltshe: rabbi's daughter; Freudienne

Ber Faytalovitsh: Smolin's discounter

Ruzhke: Ber Faytalovitsh's daughter

Khone Baker: baker

Yosl Katazhan: owner of a grain warehouse and member of Jewish community council

Itshe Shpilfoygl: timber merchant

Oyzer: butcher

Itshe Tshap: letter writer

Witbrot: German colonist, owner of the orchard

PART I

1

IT'S NOT SO BAD YET

A stillness over the soldiers' cemetery.

Among the rows of gravestones lie carved wooden crosses overgrown with thorny weeds. They wind around the communal graves in strange networks that frighten passers-by on moonlit nights. Here lie Ukrainians and Belarusian peasants alongside big-bellied Prussians with yellow mustaches; Jewish boys from cozy homes together in the same graves with hale young men from the Vienna Prater. The whole sandy hill is engulfed in a profound silence. Only in the autumn, when the biting winds pick up, do dried human bones appear, scattered over the isolated fields. Peasants gather them up in bags and mill them down by hand into meal to fertilize the soil. From time to time an old coach would stop there and a woman dressed in mourning clothes would alight. The people of Smolin know she is the paralyzed Countess come to mourn her only son.

⁖

Along the path facing the soldiers' cemetery stands the orchard of the German settler Witbrot. Inside the orchard lives Hersh Lustik from Smolin. He owns a full twenty-eight-year squatter's stake in the orchard. And now, with this new summer, he is bustling about and fixing his wagon. It's a hazy, stuffy morning. From the ponds comes the cackle of wild geese. Jewish goats graze out on the dry meadows, plucking up last year's grasses. The freshly tilled earth is redolent of warm cow manure. From the mill on the Smolin side of the road little wagons full of flour drag themselves along in the hot sun. The white dust settles soft and thick on the orchard fence, making it difficult to breathe. Hersh Lustik wanders among the wet irrigation ditches, shaking the worms out of the trees and evaluating the fruit. The pears and apples are already flowering, their little rosy-white blossoms making a soft bed underfoot, heralding abundance and a plentiful crop. Tired after a long night of standing guard in the orchard, he collapses under a pear tree and sleeps the sweet sleep that comes after a day's work. When he awakes, the sun is about to set.

"Time to head home. My wife, the worrier, will start to fret," Hersh says apprehensively.

He takes his coat down from the branches where it hung like a scarecrow, wraps a dozen odd eggs in a red kerchief, and tucks a young hen under his arm—a chicken for the Sabbath. Hopefully that would keep his wife, Ratse, from scowling for once and maybe she would greet him with a cheerful face.

Before he knows it he's made it to the green tavern. His long walking stick in hand, he strides down the narrow lanes, a tall man with a tanned, olive complexion and lively eyes under unkempt, bushy eyebrows. His salt-and-pepper beard, curled in ringlets, falls leisurely onto his chest. His gait is steady, measured. From the open windows wafts the sour smell of borsht and rye bread. That's how the people of Smolin make do during the days between Passover and Shavuot, or when made to endure some difficult period. Outside in front of their doors sit girls with their hair freshly washed—knitters who make sweaters and berets by hand to sell in the big cities.

It smells of herbage. From the whitewashed houses earthenware pots of sour milk are brought out along with fresh baked bread for the Smolin broommakers who stand around, leaning on the fences. Some of them crack sunflower seeds, while others talk about a coal strike in England, or about China. One of them, a youth with a black mane, starts strumming a mandolin. The girls listen with tender longing. From behind the acacia trees comes muffled laughter. It's a warm, carefree evening, the kind that calms one's spirits.

An outsider, Gabriel Priver, walks on the opposite side of the street. He's dressed in a linen suit and a straw hat, a pair of wrinkled gloves in his hand. The townsfolk cannot understand why one would wear gloves in the summer. Golde, a tall brunette, walks with light little steps next to him. Her dark hair is bound with a wide red ribbon. Gabriel looks to be about thirty-four or thirty-five, with a longish, bronze face, a high forehead, and deep-set blue eyes. He has the look of a man who knows his own worth and seeks no one's approval. He says something, choosing his words. An amused smile flutters over Golde's dark face. But she understands nothing of what Gabriel is talking about. She knows only one thing: Gabriel is her cousin and a full-fledged doctor. No one could reproach her for walking free and easy with a young man like that through the streets of Smolin. Even her grandfather, Yisrultshe Blimeles, doesn't say a thing. That pleasant-sounding word—*cousin*—protects her from people's malicious gossip. The townsfolk turn up their noses at Golde walking with Gabriel and shake their heads with contempt. They know this won't last long. Because Gabriel Priver, a doctor without a practice, has come to Smolin only for the summer. He is chummy with everyone and is especially close with Hersh Lustik. Gabriel stops to strike up a conversation with him.

"Good evening, Hersh. When can I come to the orchard for some plums?"

Hersh Lustik looks around the street. Young people are sitting in front of their doors and the Smolin knitters are taking it easy. Today, Thursday, is their payday. The young folk are in high spirits, which pleases him. He points his finger, cautioning them, but at the same time meaning to caution Gabriel who is walking in his dignified, cultivated way next to Golde.

"Plums? I see how it is, children. You've got no patience to wait till the fall when the plums'll be ripe. You've got a sweet tooth for plums. Take care, sweet little children, not to choke on the stones."

The girls shoot him heated glances, while young men in black tunics exchange winks, following Lustik with the mischievous looks men give, waiting for him to disappear into the market.

·∴·

What could have happened in Smolin? In the square, between the pharmacy and the town hall, little groups of well-off Jews have gathered. They speak in a whisper, looking around suspiciously and shaking their heads as though over some done deal. Opposite them, by the water pump, stand the common folk: Lazar Kurnik, the poultryman, and his associates, who are called the "Tailor-Farrier-Cobbler-Coachman Society." There they stand, brash young men holding their heads arrogantly and talking loudly. Lazar Kurnik, the eldest among them, calmly chews the corner of his little straw-colored beard. He shrugs his shoulders.

"I'm not afraid. What have I got to be afraid of? They're going to take away my vast fortunes? And a punch, that's not such a grave danger. We once served the Russians and got a taste of the whip. The world doesn't end because of a punch."

Bertshik Shmatte and Avreml "Treyf" stand in their tall boots. The leather visors of their caps shine over their red faces, full of strength and vigor. Their hands are shoved deep into their pockets. Just today Avreml "Treyf" had caused a to-do at the slaughterhouse over a remark he let slip, and as a result some affair came to light. Now he's biting his tongue, unable to stand still. But Bertshik Shmatte is the preferred speaker. When someone needs to speak, he's the one who goes first. Tsvetl, the prettiest knitter in Smolin, strolls back and forth on the sidewalk with her girlfriends. Bertshik doesn't take his eyes off her. An inner force overwhelms him and ignites his manly passions.

"Just let those turkeys try and raise a ruckus."

Golde's father, Shmuel Loyvitsher, the head of the Smolin Jewish community and a wealthy dry-goods merchant, sits on the doorstep of his shop sucking on some candy and reading the paper. Leaning on the door behind him stands his wife, Sheva, a dark, graceful woman with a small, dainty mouth, her hair bound in a flowery kerchief. Her almond eyes wander restlessly over the market, lest in the darkness she overlook a customer and her neighbor, another dry-goods dealer, snatch him up. What's more, she really wants to know where Golde had disappeared to with her cousin. That cousin's arrival in Smolin hadn't pleased Sheva at all. It's all been just a bit too grand for Golde, this having a doctor for a cousin. Then all of a sudden he's being thought of as one of the family! No, Sheva's heart tells her no good can come of it. She doesn't need any doctor cousins.

Grocers and ironmongers stand around in light jackets, smeared with oil and kerosene; short of breath and weary from hard work, they lean their ears in to hear. Shmuel Loyvitsher pushes up the glasses that keep falling down his long, sharp nose and reads aloud the description of what happened in Cyncymin. The Jews hang their heads toward the ground, listening in silence. These are the days between Passover and Shavuot. They are already up to the 17th day of counting the Omer and a gloom hangs over Smolin.[1]

Shmuel's father-in-law, Yisrultshe Blimeles, is a tall, broadshouldered old man with weak, round eyes and a brow as wrinkled as if it had been caught between the rollers of a press. Once an ambitious go-getter, now he does only what he needs to get into heaven. Yisrultshe Blimeles listens to the news with apprehension. His thin, stick-like fingers tremble. He lifts his rheumy eyes and groans hoarsely, "Oh, dear Lord in heaven, merciful Father, take pity on these few Jews of Yours, for they have become the objects of shame and humiliation. It's *no good*. This is . . . an *ug-ly* tale. It's already gone too far!" He unties the red kerchief from around his neck.

Grunem, whom everyone calls "the Long Suffering," is Yisrultshe's thirty-two-year-old son-in-law. He'd been involved in all kinds of business deals and was ultimately stuck with a wife, six children, and a broken-down buckwheat mill. Grunem stands by, looking pale, with a smooth, hairless chin. He has a sour look on his sunken face as if his ships were sinking. Among that group of Jews, every word of his sinks like a stone into black water.

"It's bad, folks, it's bad. You've got to take what you've got," he says as he eyes his six little children running barefoot around the marketplace, "and go away, wherever you get it in your heads to go. What're you waiting for?"

Hersh Lustik arrives from the orchard. With his tall frame he cuts a path through the marketplace like a bird who launches itself boldly and at an angle from the nest. He taps his stick cheerfully on the cobblestones, his long head swaying and a mocking smile playing above his salt-and-pepper beard.

"Just look at Grunem, how he's croaking and instilling fear in everyone. It's not so bad for the Jews."

The worried faces in the crowd are set momentarily at ease. Maybe it really is only an illusion, this kind of collapse. It won't last long. But Shmuel Loyvitsher quickly spoils the mood again. As the head of the Jewish community and a wealthy man, his opinion carries some weight.

"Hersh!" he declares with authority, because by nature he hates being contradicted. "Nevertheless it says so right here in the paper. Just read what's happened at the fair in Boża Wola."

Two of Hersh Lustik's long fingers pinch together and creep their way into Yisrultshe Blimeles' tobacco tin like a rooster in a stranger's coop. He dusts off his beard.

"Why can't you understand, my dear folks? After all, the ones writing for the papers are also Jews who need to make a living. The more troubles for the Jews, the more papers that get read."

Grunem's teeth begin to chatter. He grabs Lustik by the lapel.

"But Hersh, are they beating us up or aren't they? Just give me a straight answer, no pretexts."

Hersh screws up his eyes.

"They're not beating us up so hard. Just between us, when didn't they beat up on us? Sometimes a little more, sometimes a little less. It all evens out. I'm gonna give you the plain truth: Jews get the beatings they deserve. Not only that, but sometimes my own hands are itching for a go. And I'm looking at you, Shmuel. You are, as they say, really something. Our advocate. Oh, if only I could drop your pants and count out thirty-nine little lashes! 'It's bad,' Shmuel groans, 'for the Jews. It's tough for the Jews.' But will he lower the price of cloth by ten groshens a yard for the common man? Or did he, this selfsame Shmuel, go and allow the closing of the communal guest house in order to save the Jewish community another two hundred a year? It's good Smolin's got a Hersh-the-Orchard-Keeper with a spare room filled with straw, otherwise the beggars'd have to sleep out under the open skies with their wives and children. Don't go asking if the Jews are a good little people. Just give them a free hand and you'll see what they're capable of."

Grunem doesn't want to give up. All the sourness of those dark days is written on his face. His eyes, vehement in the wake of those terrible events, see images no one else sees. The badness just keeps growing. His imagination runs away with him, and Grunem has no way to keep up with it let alone stop it.

"Thank you, Hersh! God bless you, Hersh! What would you do, Hersh, if you were off somewhere and a gang of hoodlums attacked you with sticks, or poles, or iron rods, or whatever else? What would you do, hunh? Crack jokes then, would you?"

Grunem's eyes glow with a morbid terror, as if that whole imaginary gang were standing right there in front of him. But Hersh Lustik remains unimpressed. His unkempt, bushy eyebrows just keep going up and down.

"What would I do? Just you imagine that I've already done it. This little welt, here on my forehead, I got it an hour ago."

The circle of people draws tighter. Hersh Lustik stands in the middle of the crowd as they examine the blue mark on his temple. Grunem steps aside respectfully. Eyes and ears are pricked in attention. Hersh Lustik explains: "My grandpa, Nisn, the innkeeper in Boża Wola—may we all be so lucky—used to get whipped by the nobleman three times a week. Mum was the word over his quarter of veal, his half pint of brandy, and it was back to handling the nobleman's business. There weren't any newspapers then, so all he could do was put up with it in silence. Today times are different. If someone's rotten old teeth get knocked out, or if their patched shingle roof (that needs tearing off anyway) gets torn down, it's the end of the world! But now the innkeepers are gone, and so are the noblemen. So I'm walking out of the orchard and turning onto the road to Loyvitsh, when the German Witbrot calls out after me: *'Passen Sie auf, Herr Lustik, in diesem Dorfe sind Schläger da!'*—'Watch out, Herr Lustik, there are thugs in the village!' I don't say anything back to the German. I just continue on my way and think to myself: 'I know who the thug is, the real thug, the worst Haman, the oldest of all the thugs, who started the whole fire.' I come out onto the paved road, by the new brick school, when a gang of frenzied youths bursts out into the courtyard and starts fighting. When they see me they start aiming stones at me from behind the fence, just for the fun of it. So I think to myself: 'You've come to the right place.' I lift my stick and walk through the gate into the courtyard toward the group. I give one of 'em a whack on the backside, then another, but soft enough so it wouldn't cause him pain. After some panic they skedaddle. I don't waste a moment and follow them right into the school to see their teachers. Blood is trickling down my face. I don't wipe it off. Esau, you'll certainly remember, was a brute, but when he saw blood, he got confused. In short, I give those teachers a piece of my mind. 'You've got no clue,' I say, 'how to teach your oafish students manners!'"

"'You call yourselves teachers?' I say. 'You're teaching ninnies and dunces! Look how they've attacked a decent Jew and raised a welt on his forehead. Is this how you improve them? Such dignified gentlemen you are.' They just smile like fools. They offer me cigarettes and give me water to wash my wound. 'No thanks,' I say. 'Better to make sure a bunch of boys don't bite.' Their leader, the headmaster, replies, 'What a clever Jew, and no coward either! I like you, Yankl. Maybe you know how to play the cimbalom too?'

"'Don't you go smooth-talking me!' I answer him. 'The name's not Yankl, it's Hersh, and I'm no musician, I'm an orchard keeper. Get your students to play your cimbalom!'

"So that headmaster gives a whistle and calls in the troublemakers, lines them up in a row for me to identify the thugs. Don't ask. I didn't envy them, those lunkheads. They'll be wanting to avoid me next time, that's for sure, and get as far away as possible.

"Well, folks, it's getting late. My wife, the worrier, will be impatient to see me. Well then, Grunem, there was a beating. I'm telling you, it's just too late. We've shot our last wad of powder. The groaners and croakers are worse than the thugs. Grunem, get that into your head. Go home, folks, go to bed; it'll all pass. There's a time for everything. How does the verse go? *But the earth abideth forever.*" [2]

He takes his stick and sets off confidently, appearing tall and cheerful to that cluster of people standing with Lazar Kurnik at the pump.

2

GOLDE'S WORRIES

When it has gotten good and dark, and when everyone has gone off to dinner and the marketplace is empty, Golde comes out in front of her door. She is tall and takes after her mother, Sheva, in every way. Except her eyes are blue; Shmuel Loyvitsher's eyes. Her mild face, framed by thick locks of hair, is sprinkled with tiny pimples.

"Hot blood," says her mother. "My blood also went bad when I was eighteen."

The shutters are closed. Smolin is slowly drifting off to sleep. It's only in the pharmacy that an electric lamp glints with a weak, soporific light. Beyond the town the mill thrums *tsik, tsik, tsik*.

It's already quite late. Golde's glances wander longingly out over the marketplace. If only a girlfriend of hers would show up. She feels the urgent need to talk over what her cousin the doctor, Gabriel Priver, had said out there by the green tavern. Her mind has made a jumble of the little she can remember of what he said. But there's nobody there. Golde grows angry at her cousin for his pretty words; and at Baltshe, the rabbi's daughter, who shuts herself in the women's section of the synagogue with her books and interprets dreams; and at proud Ruzhke, Ber Faytalovitsh the Smolin discounter's daughter, who plays piano by candlelight.

In the gateway opposite the synagogue, Lazar Kurnik is loading chickens to transport overnight to Warsaw. Avreml "Treyf" leads a cow into the slaughterhouse, looking around furtively. Khone Baker stands in front of the door to his bakery, wrapped in a white sack for an apron, arranging the loaves and rolls so they could leaven in the cool air. The mayor, with a black band around his arm (he's still mourning his young wife) is headed home to bed in his empty house. He stops by the unbaked loaves, knocks his stick menacingly on the cobblestones, and with his finger threatens Khone that he would send a sanitary commission to his place. Then off he goes, black-banded arm and all. Golde looks around the marketplace. Wooden houses with their chimneys stand like stubborn goats, arranged around the town hall, fading into its shadows. Any minute now the town hall would break free and trample the little houses. The walls would burst and the roofs would collapse, burying everyone alive.

Among all those buildings only the restaurant of the German Schultz possesses some self-assurance. It stands there haughtily with its garish yellow façade. Inside, a hoarse phonograph rasps away, playing some new popular tune, which Schultz had had brought over from Germany. From the recess by the dry goods store comes Sheva's voice:

"Golde, Golde, time for bed. And bring in a bucket of water!"

Golde strolls one last time with her bucket through the marketplace to the pump. Hersh Lustik and his wife, Ratse, are coming towards her, carrying a basket covered with straw.

"Here you go, Lazar," Hersh Lustik says to Kurnik. "The first cherries of the year. Morellos! Drop them off at my broker's in Warsaw, on Mirowska Street."

He notices Golde at the pump and looks her over with a keen eye.

"Hey Golde, a little late for getting water. I saw where you went this evening, Goldele, and who you went there with. I'm gonna tell on you to your grandpa. Yisrultshe Blimeles' granddaughter! Well now, who'd've imagined such a thing!"

Golde pumps the water briskly. The water flows quickly. She grabs the bucket and hurries across the dark marketplace. She feels like she is being chased. She rushes into her nook, takes off her brassiere, and studies her white body in the mirror. It's clear, not a pimple on it. But Gabriel was surely thinking that if there were a couple of blemishes on her face then they'd be on her body as well. No, she'd show him that he was mistaken. But how? How could she show him she has a clear white body? Golde is at a loss. She lets down her hair, turns out the light, and covers herself with her blanket.

3

GABRIEL LONGS FOR FAMILY

What is Gabriel Priver, a doctor without a practice, doing in Smolin? Hersh Lustik is not one for subtleties, so when asked he answered:

"Gabriel Priver has come to get married. It may well be that we'll come to need him, too. Till now we've gotten along fine with Lineh the barber-surgeon. Applying cups or leeches and playing the fiddle. But these days, now that they've set up a steam mill with electricity, folks've gotten all sophisticated and have to have a doctor. In Warsaw, someone like that's as common as dirt, but in Smolin he's a novelty."

That's how Hersh Lustik explained Gabriel's stay in Smolin. But he doesn't understand nostalgia. How would a Jew like Hersh Lustik know a thing like that? Especially when Gabriel's friends in the big city—effete, uprooted people—don't understand it. It's something you feel. They sit in their cafes, in clouds of cigar smoke, with their mocking faces and judge: *Little Mazurka—done; Boża Wola—done; Smolin—done*. They talk the way blind people do about colors. He'll show them just how "done" Smolin is!

After twelve years wandering about the big city, Gabriel Priver had taken his firm pillow, packed up his medical degree in his canvas grip, and returned to Smolin. There he has found a grizzled uncle, Yisrultshe Blimeles, and his cousin Sheva with her dry-goods store and her husband, the leader of the Smolin Jewish community. His other cousin, Khashe, is blind in one eye and her husband's name is Grunem. He has a rusty hand mill, for milling buckwheat, and six children. Now he has to add Golde to this list.

For twelve years Gabriel had lived in academic lodgings and eaten in student canteens. Libraries, odd jobs, clubs, dances, female students. Once in a while he'd pick a girlfriend, and other times one would pick him. Everything flew by like a summer night's dream. Now he is an out-of-work doctor come home to his family. At night they give him a basin with a dipper for the ritual hand washing. In the morning his Uncle Yisrultshe Blimeles lends him two sets of *tefillin*: one Rashi and the other Rabbeinu Tam.[3] He could decide for himself which one he wanted. Gabriel uses the ordinary ones. On the Sabbath an *aliye* in the synagogue and a warm greeting from the rabbi.[4] Looks of esteem from every direction. Both because he's a doctor and because he's part of Yisrultshe Blimeles' family. That feeling of family that had gone dormant in Gabriel has been rekindled in the Smolin sun. He'd spend the whole day paying visits.

One visit is to his cousin Sheva. Her words contain the musical cadence of generations of Jewish mothers. But for his bashfulness, he would have nestled in her broad motherly apron. Sheva sighs constantly.

"Now, Płock is a city. If only I could be rid of Smolin and go back to Płock. I'd rather be there in the nighttime than here in this hick town during the day."

Gabriel cannot understand why Sheva dislikes Smolin so much. *He* feels really good here. It's worse, though, when he gets to his cousin Khashe's. Out the window go all the rules of hygiene that Gabriel had studied on a hungry stomach when he'd spend the night in train stations. The smoke scratches his throat.

Khashe's hoarse voice wakes up the children. Grunem never stops planning: should he marinate eggs, or dry mushrooms, or should he just go back to milling buckwheat on his rusty little hand mill? But there's a steam mill in Smolin now that's putting an end to the hand mills.

Gabriel has a lot to learn in Smolin. Uncle Yisrultshe Blimeles' seventy-five years can tell him a great deal. And the rabbi, who makes do with a cucumber and a bit of black bread—his bureau crammed with fifteen hundred notebooks filled with hand-written texts—is also a riddle to be solved. The rabbi's daughter, Baltshe, has wrinkles on her young forehead and knows all of Freud by heart. But she doesn't know how to go about getting psychoanalyzed. There's also that wonderful couple from the orchards. They call him Hersh Lustik and his wife Ratse they refer to as "Woebegone." How clever these Smoliners are! They have no idea about complexes. A "Woebegone," a "Long Suffering," and there you have it! Hersh Lustik calls Gabriel by his name.

"Good morning, Doctor Gabriel. You're just a sawbones. But I'm an orchard keeper, a tailor, I recite Psalms and I've got not kids. I'm a Priest and a Levite and a coachman."

Gabriel's days in Smolin are carefree. Everything is simple and innocent, like a child's tear. The present misfortune is exaggerated on purpose and is of little consequence. (As Hersh Lustik says, it'll pass on its own.) He lies down in the forest and stares into the blue sky, listening to the old forester's stories about Cossacks, about Jewish "spies" who'd been hanged, about the dead who pass themselves off as ghosts and demons. The forester's conscience is burdened with sins; he is tormented by nightmares.

In the evening, Gabriel wanders the soldiers' cemetery. *"Here Lie Thirty German Warriors, 1915." "Eighty-Three Russian Soldiers, Fallen in 1916." "Yosl Szmaragd, Soldier of the Modlin Regiment."* And in the middle, the communal grave, fenced with wire: *"Six Hundred and Fifty-Three, Fallen 1917."*

How clever Smolin surely must be to have seen and survived everything they have. Now it's quiet in the soldiers' cemetery.

Crosses and Stars of David stand next to one another surrounded by sandy vegetation. The red raspberries in the cemetery are shriveling away. No one wants to eat them. Their redness reminds people too much of blood. Gabriel sets back up one of the crosses that the wind had knocked over and fixes the wire fence so the pigs can't cavort inside.

He braids a little wreath of wildflowers and sets off back into town. It's a white night just like the one that Friday when he arrived in Smolin, worn out from looking around in vain for a medical practice in Warsaw. Sabbath candles had already been lit by the time the bus made its stop in the marketplace. He was shown to his cousin Sheva's. Golde was standing in the doorway, her hair glistening with the shimmer of dark flame. His appearance caused a pearly smile to spread across her face. A smile like that comes around once in a lifetime. His heart skipped a beat and his pulse started racing. It became quite clear to him what he, Gabriel Priver, the doctor without a practice, was going to do in Smolin.

4

GRUNEM FIXES HIS LITTLE
BUCKWHEAT MILL

I t's not true that after thirty-five years in Smolin Grunem
could just fend off his troubles and croak at misfortune. But
show Grunem a smile or a cheerful face, or as soon as he hears a
pleasant word, then that sour face of his would brighten and his
eyes would say: *Bless you, you've given me some comfort.* After what
had happened to Hersh Lustik, who got through it in one piece,
Grunem feels as if a great weight has been lifted off of him. In his
mind, what could be worse than getting beaten up? And for all
that, Smolin is still Smolin. At least, that's how one person sees
things. It all depends on the person. Some might say that it's not
for us to endure misfortune. And while some want things to be
different, it's still unbearable. He would have been a bad husband if he didn't tell his wife, Khashe, that all was still not
doomed, that the Jews were not lost yet. But as soon as he sets
foot inside the door the well of his words of consolation runs
dry. Khashe doesn't want to hear a word of it. She is knee-deep

in housework. Waging a war with the children. Shloymele and Zlatke are bickering over a couple of sour currants that they had snatched from grandpa's garden, out from under the watchful eyes of Yisrultshe Blimeles and old Zisl. Khashe wipes her face with her apron. When she bends over, her breasts hang down like two empty bellows. She lays into Shloymele with her fists:

"Killer, murderer, what are you trying to do to Zlatke? Give her the currants. Here's your father. Survived to make it home, did you? Just look at how that sonny boy of yours has scratched me up. Grunem, you've given me a houseful of children. Praise God for that. But their little stomachs are so empty they're eating unripe currants. What great success today, oh helplessmate of mine?"

Grunem stands there befuddled. He looks at her sooty face, at the naked bits of her body showing through her blouse, and he is once again plagued by doubts: If there weren't any beatings, would *that* be better? No, there are worse things than beatings.

"Khashe," he shakes his smooth, hairless face. "You've gotten some kind of mania into your head. You really do think there's nothing more important than the stomach. Come here, let me tell you what's happened in Cyncymin."

Tears well up in Khashe's blind eye as it looks at the wall though meaning to look at Grunem.

"And what good does it do me to have the community's worries on my head when I've got you to provide for me? It'd be a disgrace, God forbid, for me to have to live on welfare. Take anybody else and just look at what he'd do—run off to the village and bring back some groats for *kasha* is what. Ask Hersh Lustik to go see the mayor, maybe he'll be able to persuade him. He'll say something like: *Panie Mayor, it's dark days. Forgive Grunem's taxes and let him make a living again milling buckwheat on his hand mill.* And all with a laugh, the way Hersh Lustik can. After all, he's buddy-buddy with the mayor. Don't ask. I was happy once with a husband like that. Whatever he was worth, he's now dead and buried."

Grunem tugs at his bare chin and looks deeply into Khashe's face. Her wrinkles are no more than an illusion. Underneath the wrinkles her skin is fresh and smooth. Now, on this early summer evening, Grunem is beset by a longing for Khashe's warm body, a longing reminiscent of what he'd felt ten years earlier, before Khashe began birthing their six children. He watches her yearningly.

"Khashe, just look how we're of the same mind! We're thinking the same thought. It's not the end of the world, Khashe. Groats'll get brought from the village, the buckwheat'll get milled. And, don't you know, I'm fine with getting an allowance from your sister; she'll be able to lord it over us later. Poor things like us to live off others' gifts! They've got a girl to marry off, as Sheva says, so they're not allowed to touch Golde's dowry. May the hand wither that would take even a single groschen of it! Khashe, have you no shame in front of the children! Your naked body's hanging out. Button up your blouse!"

Grunem strokes her bosom.

Khashe loses her temper, "Foolish man! Trying to get things going. He can . . ."

Grunem's limbs are getting warm. He rubs his hands together, rolls up his sleeves, and gathers up his tools.

"Shloymele, get the saw and the hammer out from under the bed. Come to the entryway and we'll get to work. Quicker, Shloymele, quicker. It's getting late."

5

HERSH LUSTIK PAYS THE MAYOR A CONDOLENCE CALL

On Sunday, after church has let out, Hersh Lustik puts the cover on his sewing machine, dons his shiny green holiday kapote, and goes to pay the mayor of Smolin a visit. It's Smolin's *odpust* festival, the annual fair when people come from all around to have their sins absolved. The marketplace is full of non-Jews from the villages. The pump is surrounded by padded carts with colorful canopies. Respectable-looking youths in white caps have travelled from far away to wander around with earnest faces and hand out leaflets. They don't speak; they just act as if they're noble gentry, winking at one another. The peasants look at the leaflets with their humorous drawings and stick them into their bootlegs. Booths slapped together for the occasion from rough-hewn boards line either side of the market-place. "New customers for Smolin's tax office," Hersh Lustik thinks. "They'll have something others'll take. All the money they've got hidden in their socks suddenly appears so it can be invested in some new deal or other. The marketplace is bursting with merchandise, but there are no buyers to be seen." Hersh Lustik makes his way through the village crowd. He's a full head taller than those stunted peasants. Pranksters from the tailors' quarter, drunken brickmakers and the knackers' boys who like to play all kinds of tricks on the people of Smolin, all seem to want to pick fights with Hersh, ridiculing his vented kapote and making sport of its coattails. Hersh Lustik shoots them daggers with his mischievous eyes, whispering to himself: *"God said to Jacob, 'Fear thou not, O my servant Jacob'."*[5]

The snooty brickmakers with their foolishly upturned noses are left standing stunned as Hersh Lustik continues on his way. He nods at familiar gentiles, asking after their winter planting, their meadows of strewn hay, their cows ready for calving. In this way, he walks with his playful gait into Boża Wola Street. Jews are standing around their own booths, on the left-hand side, away from the church. A bit further on and up, among the expansive maples, stands the long, blushing red-brick house of the mayor. The white shutters are shut from the inside, so Hersh stands for some time in the semicircular stone doorway, not knowing what to do. Hersh knows that this is a mourning custom. The mayor is still grieving for his young wife who was taken from this world in childbirth. His wife's death has affected him deeply, and he re-solved never to marry again. It's still a good deed to console him, even though he's a non-Jew. He is good to the Jews, and is simply an honest gentile. Had it been up to the mayor, Soreh-Gitl's son, Moshke, would not have been packed off to prison and Grunem's burdensome taxes would have been relieved.

He knocks, quietly, as if the mayor's wife were still lying ill in bed and mustn't be woken up. From inside he hears the soft padding of slippered feet. The mayor himself opens the door. In the gap of the open door the mayor's head appears, over-grown with snow-white stubble, his eyes red and swollen. The mayor has aged greatly over the past few days. A broken man. Hersh Lustik extends his hand to him warmly. The mayor's stony face perks up.

"Ah, it's you, Hershek. It's just, I thought . . . What did I think? I'm so woozy these days. Come in, Hershek! It's not so tidy, I'm afraid. I let the maids go; you see, Hershek, what do I need them for? Franciszka's gone. Everything can just go to hell."

Hersh Lustik is deeply moved. A gentile soul wallowing in such misery. He looks into the mayor's eyes.

"You mustn't think that way, Wojtuś. It's sinful. A person must be prepared to accept all things and not fall into despair. Follow our example. That's exactly why I've come, Wojtuś. It's a custom among the Jews. It's called *menakhem ovl*, 'comforting the mourner.' Let yourself be comforted, Wojtuś. We go back a long ways. We used to chase pigeons together as boys, playing around in the clay pits."

The mayor's pale face begins to flush. He grasps Hersh Lustik's hand.

"What did you call it, Hershek, *'manakhe abel'*? So that's what you call a comforting word: *'manakhe abel'*. I can understand that. It's all so different for you Jews. It has real meaning. My friends stayed with me the whole night eating and drinking till they almost burst. While my poor Franciszka was standing, alive, right before my eyes and this funeral meal seemed repulsive, as if worms were eating her body . . . Among you Jews, one's allowed to be sad. Come here, Hershek, let's have a little drink. We once played together, you said. Well, we're a couple of decrepit old men now. Neither of us have any children. When you consider that your little world ends with you, that it's all finished . . . Oh, Franciszka, Franciszka. Why did you do this? To die and take our child with you. Come, drink, Hershke. *'Manakhe abel'* you say? To hell with it all . . ."

They move over to a small sitting room and sit down at a little mahogany table, puffing on their pipes. The mayor casts fretful glances at the picture hanging, covered, over the sideboard. He leans over toward Hersh and whispers in his ear:

"You see, Hershek, I was afraid she'd come at night to strangle me so I had that picture covered up. She came to me in a dream the other night. She was standing by the door in a shirt that reached down to her ankles, silent, with accusation in her eyes. She never spoke a word, but those eyes of hers . . . If you had seen those eyes . . . *Murderer*, they said, *you took me from this world. Give me back my child*. Then she burst into tears; she came over to me and started caressing me: 'Wojtuś, Wojtuś, my husband!' I wanted to take hold of her, embrace her, hug her, but she melted away in my arms recoiling into a shadow. 'I am no longer yours,' she said. 'You mustn't touch me.' My heart could have burst, Hershek. What did you call it, *'manakhe abel'*? Ah, Jews, Jews . . . Such a clever people. The Devil won't take you."

He pours a glass of slivovitz and drains it. The color returns to his face. He grows cheerful and gives Hersh a hearty slap on the knee. His voice sounds confident, almost mocking.

"Hershek, when are you going off to Palestine? People say that by New Year's half of the Jews will have left Smolin. When you get to Palestine, Hershek, you should go to Bethlehem and drop in on my brother, Wacek. He's done alright for himself, that Wacek. Never knew what a wife is. Lives peacefully in the church, and every day gets to see God's cradle, the manger. When are you hitting the road, Hershek?"

Hersh stretches out comfortably in the soft, padded armchair and takes a long, lazy yawn.

"Wojtuś, I'm not going anywhere. I'm staying here."

The mayor, who's already a little animated, jumps angrily out of his seat. He stands there for a moment on tottering feet before falling back down into his armchair.

"You're not going, Hershek? When all the Jews are going, you alone are going to stay? Where will you pray, Hershek? Do you think that just for your sake I'm going to leave the *mikveh* so the young mischief-makers can go peeking at the women? [6] I'll order both the *mikveh* and the synagogue be dismantled. They're on the verge of collapse as it is. I'll do it, I'll do it for sure."

Hersh bursts out laughing.

"Dear Wojtuś, you're still the same old person. Thinking just like when we were kids. Not all of the Jews are going. Whoever wants to go will go. And whoever prefers to stay will stay. These are individual choices; no one's being forced."

The mayor twirls his mustaches up, little fires flickering in his eyes.

"You, Hershek. You permit yourself too many liberties with the mayor. You think that because my Franciszka has died and you've come here to '*manakhe abel*' that means you can say anything? I'll put your case on trial, Hershek! It seems you've had your say. Just wait a moment. What did you say? That you, Hershek, can stay in Smolin? To hell with that. There are still a few honest Jews I know—Srulek Blimeles, Shmulek from Loyvitsh, Berek Faytalovitsh the discount agent who lent money to the city government. But the rest, the beggars, let them go. Oh, Franciszka, Franciszka, if only I were twenty-five years younger . . ."

Hersh just sits, calmly inhaling the smoke. He smiles right at the mayor.

"Wojtuś, you're like a cask of beer whose foam sprays out when you open it, then, once it's left for a bit, goes flat. It's not going to do you any good. We Jews must live together with you in Smolin. That's how it's been since time immemorial. Ask yourself, Wojtuś, what does a Jew need? Jews are like birds on God's green earth. They don't need much: a little seed, a little feather, a little nest; but we get to eat challah on the Sabbath. Wojtuś, leave the Jews in peace. Just remember how I dragged you out of that pond when you nearly drowned. Were it not for me, you wouldn't be mayor today."

"It really would have been better that way, Hershek. Why *did* you drag me out of the water that day? You damned yid. It's because of you that Franciszka departed this world so young, you devil . . . Come here, let's drink another glass." He grabs Hersh by the sleeve. "What a loathsome thing it is, Hershek, to live all alone on God's green earth. What good does Palestine do you, Hershek? Stay here! Is it really so bad for you among us? You can keep leasing those little orchards to your heart's content. You've got a synagogue to pray in, right? And you eat *tsimmes* on the Sabbath? Where will you drag your meager bones off to in your old age? What's true is true. It's very distressing to hear those people chiding you. But that Jewish doctor, that *Pan* Gabriel Priver, is a good person. He explained everything about Franciszka's departing this world. Hershek, we're of an older generation; we don't understand people today. Don't let what they say bother you. Just think of it as the wind whistling in the chimney. Humor an old friend, stay! Let's have another couple of glasses. It's good you came to '*manakhe abel*' me. Oh, Franciszka, Franciszka . . ."

Through the open window comes the odor of the fertilized fields of Smolin. The sun is sinking into the Vistula. It has already dipped into the western horizon. Shadows are dancing on the walls of the sitting room. Both men are silent, lost in memories of their long-ago childhoods on that fertile earth.

6

TWO KINDS OF WORRY

Yisrultshe Blimeles has played his life's last card. His old age seems like the prolonged interim days of one of the week-long festivals. He remembers what the early days looked like. Those were his first seventy-five years, which he had spent in wealth and respect. The latter days—those are the world on the other side of Smolin, a whole new world. Yisrultshe Blimeles had given charity and done good deeds his whole life. But how have things gone the last couple of years? No one leaves him in peace. On one side there's Khashe, his daughter with her six children and that hopeless failure of a husband, Grunem. They chip away at him as much as they can, tearing off whole living chunks. On the other side his Jewish troubles plague him. They are embittering his final days. What's more, a resentment towards God has taken hold of him—why couldn't He have waited a couple more years to afflict the Jews with such misfortunes so that he, Yisrultshe, might not have had to see what he was seeing.

In the late morning he heads home from the synagogue with his big *tallis*-bag under his arm,[7] taking measured steps and stopping every couple of minutes to take a breather. He sees the world working the way it's used to working. People pair up, occupy themselves with the business of this world. Children arrive (no Evil Eye) in the gutters of the Smolin marketplace. The commandment to be fruitful and multiply is never for a minute impeded among the Jews, even though a hint comes from on high: *Jews, stop your multiplying.* Ber Faytalovitsh, the Smolin discounter, wearing his shiny chamois boots, approaches Yisrultshe and bids him a hearty, respectful greeting. But there's something disdainful in that greeting, the way one salutes an old, retired general. Ber, absorbed in his earthly affairs, climbs into his little yellow britzka and sets off for the squire's estate. There's money to be made there.

Next to Yosl Katazhan's house (nobody knows how he's suddenly achieved such prominence) stands a long line of wagons loaded with logs, which reminds Yisrultshe of his youth. He, too, had once dealt in the wood trade. Foolishness. If his eyesight were better he'd take up the book of Ecclesiastes again. Everything is there in the book of Ecclesiastes.

He pops into the bakery. Khone Baker, swaddled with a sack as always, is sitting by the sideboard, dunking a stale roll into his coffee. He stands and offers Yisrultshe a chair. Yisrultshe takes his wallet out of his pocket, holds it up to his left eye, and rummages around for a long while with his bony fingers.

"Here you go, Khone. Here's for Khashe's six loaves. Just don't let on; I don't want the wife to know. After all, Zisl's a stepmother. Khone, you sleep through the days that God's granted to the world; but at night, Khone, at night you make it all right again by making people's bread! It's an important thing, Khone. It maintains the survival of the world!"

Khone Baker jumps, scattering the flour from his clothes thickly over the shop and making it difficult for Yisrultshe to breathe.

"Yisrultshe, you have accomplished far more in this world. I'm only a common baker, a simple person; what do I know of higher things beyond the dough-kneading trough? Now the mechanical ovens have issued their decree. I'll give Khashe her bread. You didn't want the match, Yisrultshe. She'd have been happy with me. But I'm not worthy of being your son-in-law, Yisrultshe."

Yisrultshe Blimeles isn't listening. He continues on his way and is panting heavily by the time he stops at Sheva's dry goods store. He calls inside to his son-in-law:

"Shmuel! Have they brought the paper yet? People're saying Hitler's already made another speech, eh?"

Shmuel Loyvitsher isn't particularly happy to have to come outside. His father-in-law is probably bothering him because he has a hankering for a snack. But Shmuel holds his tongue. He calls over Shloymele, Grunem's boy, who is playing in his bare feet by the water, wearing a threadbare little kapote.

"Shloymele, get yourself over to Yosl Katazhan's for the paper!" Turning to Yisrultshe, "He's become a newspaperman, that Katazhan. If you need the paper, there aren't any. Pretends he's reading it."

Yisrultshe Blimeles leans in closer.

"What? Are you talking about Hitler?"

"I'm talking about Yosl Katazhan. Wants to be a councilman. He's been hanging onto that paper a bit too long."

"Ah, Yosl Katazhan. What did Hitler say?"

Shmuel Loyvitsher bursts out laughing.

"You and your Hitler. It's all Hitler this and Hitler that. We've got more pressing problems right here."

Yisrultshe blinks his purblind eyes.

"The slaughter, eh? No help for it. Not destined to live out these final years in peace."

He gets up to get a bite to eat. As is his habit, he drops a coin into the alms box. Glancing over the leaflets from the yeshivot tacked up in a jumble over the bureau he takes a powder for his heart and heads back down to his place to inspect his estate.

He creeps austerely among the rooms and stables, considering the wooden compartments. Here a window broken, there a door hinge missing, and the gate to the garden stands open.

Khashe's children, in tattered clothes and covered in mud, are milling about in the garden as if it were a zone of lawlessness. They pick raspberries, pluck unripe cherries from the trees, and run riot over the flowerbeds.

"What children!" Yisrultshe Blimeles thinks. "In difficult times like these. The world trembles and they just keep on doing what they're doing. Maybe that's the wisdom of the world. One can learn a thing or two from children. Life is preferable to anything else."

He takes out his red handkerchief and waves it at them.

"Don't go getting yourselves hurt! Out, you little devils! You're trampling the garden. Grandma Zisl will see and then she'll really let you have it."

Shloymele, his face smeared red with raspberry, grabs a handful of pea pods, creeps up onto the fence, and wags his little finger, "*Be-e-eh*, grampa!"

Yisrultshe, feeling tired, sits down on the chaise, breathing with difficulty.

"Such little devils, making a ruin of the garden. In such times . . ."

All at once he starts picking at his nose. Then a sneezing fit. A heavy odor has upset his asthma.

In the slimy water trickling in the ditch through the garden Yisrultshe Blimeles spies a pair of stony green eyes. His cat lies dead in the stagnant muck, stretched out like a corpse after its ritual purification. Yisrultshe stands there, stunned. He takes a good long look at the cat. A creature, like all creatures. But what would become of it after death! Once again he thinks of the book of Ecclesiastes. If he could catch Shloymele, he'd twist his ear. That's his job.

"Yech, what a stench!" Yisrultshe says and continues on his way.

He spots Golde behind a pear tree. She is lying on the grass, her face buried in a book, fanning her bare legs. Yisrultshe stands still, his mouth gaping, with a look on his face like someone had just insulted him.

"Is that really you? Have you no shame, a young woman of marriageable age lying on her belly? Cover your legs!"

Golde jumps up, blushing, and pulls her dress over her knees. She hangs her head.

"Good morning, grampa."

"Good morning. So what's got you so engrossed? What've you got there?"

"A book, grampa."

"Oh, books, books," Yisrultshe groans. "Do books fortify you in times such as these? Better to take a copy of *Hemdat Shlomo* for women, or the *Sefer ha-Yashar* in Yiddish.[8] Goldele, Goldele, you're already of marrying age."

Golde plucks at the tassels of her jacket.

"Grampa, I want to go to Warsaw."

Yisrultshe's weak eyes blink. His forehead, wrinkled like a washboard, rises with concern.

"To Warsaw? What would you do there, in that Warsaw? What are big cities good for? And you a young girl . . ."

"Grampa, I want to find a job in a store, as a shop girl or a cashier."

Yisrultshe shakes his head in astonishment.

"A shop girl, a shop girl . . . Working with those people. Are you missing something at home? We've seen the great things that can be accomplished in those cities. Take your cousin Gabriel, for example. A doctor, eh? He walks around in ratty shoes! Don't go changing places, Golde. Don't dishonor Smolin. If it's our destiny, Smolin will again be restored. People from the big cities will come *here*. That's for certain."

"But Grampa, it's boring here in Smolin."

Yisrultshe caresses her cheek, as a little condescending smile spreads across his face.

"Silly child. What does that mean that you're bored? You'll find a husband, you'll have children, you'll be a proper Jewish wife. There are enough miseries waiting for you. Your boredom will come to an end soon enough."

Golde grabs him by the hand.

"I want to go away, Grampa. I don't want to be here."

Yisrultshe gives her a little slap on her bare knee.

"What do you mean, 'you want'? You have a mother and a father for as long as they live. *They* get to want for you. Only bad things come from children wanting for themselves. Going off on new paths and not looking after their parents' welfare."

Sheva's voice comes from the office, "Golde, where've you gone off to again? There's a couple of customers in the shop. Go and fetch a pitcher of water."

Golde throws on her scarf. Excusing herself from her grandfather she sets off for the pump in the marketplace.

Yisrultshe sits down on a tree stump. He feels a tightness in the top of his stomach, and he has the hiccups from the stale pastry he had eaten for a snack. He breathes heavily. In the distance the Smolin mill is panting along with him.

7

SMOLIN HEALS

Where is Gabriel Priver going to hang out his shingle? In front of Ber Faytalovitsh's place there's a little flower garden. Gabriel remembers that garden from his childhood. It marks off Ber Faytalovitsh's house from the rest of Smolin. Gabriel had never gone further than the stairs. Behind the curtains it smells of cloves and the smoke of gentlemanly cigars. Inside there are fine rugs, carved furniture, silver. Gabriel knows these are now all as good as kindling for the fire. The biggest piece of kindling is the old-fashioned grand piano that Faytalovitsh had bought at auction at the Smolin manor. There the black instrument stands in its Smolin confinement, dreaming of its childhood, of manorial comfort and the rustle of silk dresses. For whole weeks the piano remains stubbornly silent. But once in a while of a Sabbath morning as the townsfolk lie sunk in their honest, carefree Sabbath sleep, the piano would suddenly burst to life from its torpor, its keys hurriedly dancing with angry notes as though a thunderstorm were descending on Smolin. Soon the skies would clear. The waters would ebb. Submissive chords would echo softly.

"Ruzhke's rebelling against her father. She's going to turn into a spinster. No rich man's going to begrudge anyone that dowry of hers. Even a nobleman won't pay his debts!" So grumble the wagging tongues of Smolin for having been woken from their sleep.

It's not so easy for Gabriel to hang out his white medical shingle. Beyond Smolin lies Big Mazurka where the starosta lives.[9] It's up to him whether Smolin would be permitted a doctor by the name of Gabriel Priver or whether Smolin would do without a doctor at all, as it had till then. But whoever wants to live on credit must learn to bend a little at certain moments—a bit of wisdom Gabriel Priver had learned from his student days. By virtue of his meekness Gabriel had taken his degrees. Life's harsh realities had hardened him, so he was able to get the better of those who demanded his submission.

Now his doctor's shingle hangs on Ber Faytalovitsh's wall. It looks out, shy and unassuming, over the Smolin marketplace. In that modesty lies Gabriel Priver's pride, one that tells of long years of tenacious hard work and commitment to self-discipline. But no patients have come. Endurance is required. So Gabriel sits in the old rocking chair that he borrowed from Shmuel Loyvitsher, the head of the Smolin community and Golde's father, and listens to the piano music coming from the other side of the wall. The chords reach him muted, as if coming from underground. They speak to him of repressed feminine emotions, of masculine thirst for gold, the things that devour young lives.

Gabriel wants to drive out these painful thoughts. He closes the window and heads out into the marketplace. He walks with confident steps over the hard earth. For Smolin is no ethereal, ephemeral thing. Uncle Yisrultshe Blimeles is like an oak that the wind might lash and strip of its leaves but could not uproot. Golde is also a part of that landscape. She is as raw and simple as the earth of Smolin. It was from that same earth that he, Gabriel Priver, had sprung. And it was here that he had returned. He would ask the people of Smolin: *Am I to blame for being a doctor? Must I atone for my years in the big city, out of touch with the music of my family? Heedless of the joyful melody that is Golde's mother's laughter? Deaf to the fact that when Khashe with the blind eye cries it also has a melody, only a sad one?* Gabriel is dying for a melody. In Bertshik Shmatte, who gets drunk in Schultz's restaurant and picks fights with peasants, there is a longing, the generations-long yearning of untapped strength. In the evening, that longing dissipates over the orchards of Smolin, filling Gabriel's heart with mildness and goodwill to all men. He hears leisurely, staccato footsteps behind him.

"Good morning, Doctor! 'Michael to my right, Gabriel to my left.' [10] Stubborn people in Smolin. Don't wanna be sick. They *are* sick, but they'll begrudge their doctor any pleasure from their sickness. Every man seeks his livelihood. Go on, Doctor, get yourself some patients. No one's gonna make your living for you," Hersh Lustik says to Gabriel's back, and, not waiting for an answer, continues on his way.

Gabriel wouldn't be able to get by without sick patients. But his mind has gone to sleep. His hands are idle. Gabriel needs wounds and diseased limbs to heal. He needs cries of joy; he misses people's sighs. He doesn't notice how it is he's reached Grunem's house. Its two little rooms are suffused with the family smell of early morning untidiness. Straw litter, pillow feathers, and stained sheets lie about the floor. Khashe runs up to him, her hair disheveled, wiping off a bench with her apron and patting his arm.

"Here, sit, darling Gabriel. Would you look at that, you're a doctor and still not embarrassed to come visit your poor cousin. Sit, sit, silly boy. Grunem, why're you just lying there on the bench? Go get a bottle of kvass. You've come on a regular day; we've got nothing to treat you with."

Grunem climbs down off his bench and offers Gabriel a hospitable greeting.

"My foot's hurting today, may it not happen to you, so I've had to lie down for a bit."

"Yeah, right, your foot," Khashe shakes her head at Grunem, seeing right through her partner. "That foot of his has clobbered me, nearly ruined me. If not for that foot, what could've been."

Grunem responds in the same allusive language, "Enough. You're starting that again? Why's your cousin need to know about that?"

Khashe digs in her heels. "Of course he should know. Everybody should know how deep my ruin is."

Gabriel sizes Grunem up with his doctorly eye.

"Just show me that foot of yours and let me take a look."

Grunem's hairless face turns as red as a copper pan. He stammers something, and in that stammering Khashe hears some teeth grinding.

"An open wound, not fresh."

Khashe concedes, "The wound's been open since before the wedding. He hid it from me. As soon as it starts raining that wound of his opens."

"A wound needs to be treated. Grunem, show me your foot."

Something's choking inside Grunem, simmering in him like a covered pot on the boil. His eyes shoot sparks at Khashe. He turns back to Gabriel and asks in a gentle voice, "Why should our cousin trouble himself with it? It's an old story. From my cantonist days. Not worth the effort."

Khashe's watchful eyes well up, "Good then, at least you're ashamed. More and more like your father. Pretended to be a miserable cripple. When you go serve then I'll be happier."

Gabriel examines Grunem's wound: a deep, longish cut, hollowed out like a small boat. The wound is dark and oozing a fluid that gives off an acrid smell. Gabriel's alarmed eyes range from Grunem to Khashe, and from Khashe to their children.

"It could be gangrene, blood poisoning."

A wry smile appears on Grunem's pale face. "Gangrene, shmangrene. Our cousin's still a young doctor. I've aged with my wound longer than with my wife. I've no intention to go 'healing.' Just gonna live out my last few years."

Gabriel shrugs his shoulders. "Negligent people. You've got to fix what's broken. Come to my office, Grunem. We'll see if there's something that can be done. What's the matter with that little one crawling on the floor? Her belly doesn't look good to me. Her pallor."

Little Hadassah shuffles across the room toward her mother on splayed, crooked legs and hides in the folds of her apron. Khashe pushes her towards Gabriel.

"Go on, Hadassah. Uncle's going to give you something. Stand up now. Show uncle that you can walk."

Gabriel takes hold of the child's little leg and feels her bones. Hadassah bursts into tears.

Khashe's watchful eyes well up once again, "I knew it. It's the English disease, right?"[11]

"Cod-liver oil with a few drops of *vitavit*," Gabriel says with doctorly matter-of-factness. He then writes his first prescription in Smolin and hands it to Zlatke. "Take this to the pharmacy."

Zlatke examines the prescription, reading aloud from the letterhead: *Doctor Gabriel Priver.* She looks to her mother, awaiting her direction.

Khashe takes the slip of paper out of her hand and sticks it in the bosom of her dress.

"We'll buy it some other time, when things are better. So tell me, dear little Gabriel, how're things going for you here in Smolin? Got a lot of patients do you?"

Half of Gabriel's face laughs. The other half is paying no attention to Khashe.

"For the moment I have two patients."

Khashe's face takes on a serious expression.

"Praise God for that. As long as you've made a start. With God's help, Gabriel, you won't be wanting for patients. People are starved for a doctor."

Gabriel rummages through his pockets and pulls a silver coin out of his vest pocket, which he gives to Zlatke, "Take this; go to the pharmacy and buy the cod-liver oil."

Khashe runs over to Zlatke and grabs the coin out of her hand.

"I won't hear of it, Gabriel. May my hands wither if I take that."

Gabriel doesn't hear her. He closes the door behind him.

In the yard he runs into Yisrultshe Blimeles. Yisrultshe smiles at the sight of his nephew. "Well now, you're just the one I'm looking for. Truth be told, I was just going to Faytalovitsh's to take a look at that place of yours."

Soon his tone changes. A deep concern spreads over his wrinkled brow.

"Another Jew was stabbed in the Land of Israel. So, what do you say to that, Gabriel? After all, you're some kind of a doctor. Looking pretty, eh? Of course Khashe has cried her eyes out at you. You're family, so you've a right to know the truth: I'm over-doing it by indulging all of it. Naturally, you've got to consider that my old woman, Zisl, is no more than a stepmother. As I'm obviously an energetic man, I give Khone Baker three zlotys a week just for bread so those kids of Khashe's won't starve to death. And all without the old woman knowing. So I ask you: who is capable of doing that nowadays? Such a young man to in-habit these old bones! I'm telling you in all honesty, I'm not even sparing my health. I'm going to need you to write a new prescrip-tion for my heart powder. And my old woman, poor thing, is also going to need some medicine. She's got a boil under her arm. I try to comfort her: 'Better a boil on the outside than on the in-side.' But what good are my efforts when she's constantly pick-ing at that boil? It's three days already that she's laid there, groaning. I know that if you could just go up and take a look she'd probably improve. You're a doctor, after all. Negligent people, eh?"

Gabriel leaves Uncle Yisrultshe standing there in the gate; in a few strides he's already reached their floor.

8

OLD ZISL WANTS
TO ENJOY LIFE

"Excuse me, Cousin, please, *Monsieur* Doctor, pardon the disorderliness. I am not today in complete health."

The eighty-three year old Zisl looks at herself in the mirror hanging by the bed, underneath the portrait of the Magid of Kozhenits.[12] She smoothes out a lock of hair that's visible from underneath her wig.

"Yisrultshe, give me the georgette counterpane to cover the bed. Eh, Yisrultshe, no georgette? You know, *Panie* Gabriel, your uncle never comes home from synagogue for lunch before twelve. I have, you'll forgive me, a boil under my arm that keeps me up all night. I have applied linseed oil. Never in my life have I made use of a doctor. Still my own teeth, *Herr* Cousin. Only one time was I ever sick in my life, as a girl, erysipelas. Till then I had been enrolled in Gymnasium in Płock. Then the uprising broke out and there were no doctors to be had. An aunt treated me with, you'll forgive me, cow manure. *Ach!* Cousin, how it hurts under my arm. You know, my stepdaughter, Khashe, has deprived me of half my life. But you give and give and, you'll forgive me, it's a sack full of holes. And what a mouth she has! She can talk your ear off. The children are exactly like her. That Shloymele, there is not a soul in the world like him. 'Old bat' he calls me. And go sustain them on seven rolls a week. Just the other day he threw, you'll forgive me, a dead cat into my house. Ruined the preserves. *Ja, Herr* Cousin, I have six snakes hanging over my *Kopf* and she, Khashe, is the seventh snake. This boil has lasted long enough, *Herr* Doctor. If only this abscess would burst."

Gabriel washes his hands. Zisl turns to face the wall, taking out an old box of Coty from behind the pillow and hurriedly powdering her face.

"So it is in this little town, *Herr* Cousin. I would still like to see a bit of the world. To attend the opera in Warsaw. To see a film. To visit the royal palace. To enjoy life a little."

Gabriel approaches the bed. Zisl, uncovered, bashfully closes her eyes, "*Ach, Mutter!* I have pains, *Herr* Doctor. Not so hard!"

"Not much longer, Aunt," Gabriel smiles and writes a prescription. "It will last only a day or two more. Apply the ointment. No more linseed oil."

Now calm, Zisl hides the prescription under her pillow the way one squirrels away what might one day be useful but isn't needed at present. She opens an envelope of photographs, her white, powdered face beaming with joy.

"Have a look, *Herr* Cousin, at these splendid pictures! My offspring from my first consort. This one is a lawyer in New York. His son studies medicine. This niece is a famous pianist. *So, so,* my friend. In America one can raise one's children to achieve their goals. Smolin is no city. Either one tends a store, or one tends an orchard, or one tends children."

"America, America—you know what? I wouldn't offer you *ten* Americas for one Holy Land!" Yisrultshe Blimeles says, catching his breath in the doorway.

Seized by a fit of coughing he sits down in a green frayed armchair, panting heavily and in time with the steam mill.

"The butcher . . ."—here he starts coughing again—". . . the butcher just read in the *Togblat* that they defiled the Western Wall with excrement. So I ask you, Gabriel, since you're so learned in the affairs of the world, how long will the Arabs continue running amok? Will the boil disappear on its own, eh? The one insult to add to my injury would be my wife being sick. Our neighbor across the way, Soreh-Gitl, the poor thing, is dying. A heart condition (may we be spared). She has only one son, Moshke, who's sitting in prison. What a deluded boy: he was going to change the world! Coming to Smolin, Gabriel, you were always going to get the worst of it all. They've made do without a doctor; but having finally caught the scent of one, they're all going to want treatment. All of Smolin is a single wound. Maybe you'd like to pop in on our neighbor and just have a look? Here's Ratse now, Hersh Lustik's wife. She's related to Soreh-Gitl. A sister. Oh, *tsar gidul bonim*, the travails of raising children. Such a boy, nowadays, to go and incite a world . . ."

"Soreh-Gitl's at death's door. The pain has moved to her liver," Ratse says.

Her face is smooth and fresh, but a deep distress hovers over it. Maidenly guilelessness shelters in her eyes.

"Y'can take a seat," Yisrultshe gestures toward Ratse with his hand, not looking at her.

"I didn't come to sit, Zisl dear. I heard the doctor was here. Hersh told me, 'Go invite the doctor. He's a dependable sort, with a Jewish mind.' What more is there to say? Soreh-Gitl is well cared for. The sick man's in pain wherever you put him. With kids it's bad, without them it's worse. She's been a widow for seven months now. Her eldest, Tsvetl, the knitter, is made miserable by those sweaters, toiling non-stop for the agent. Pesele's still in school. She's just a child, after all. I'll take her with me to the orchard. Moshke, well, you all know the dirty trick *he* played on his parents. Doctor, when your family wants to be good, well . . . Go look in on Soreh-Gitl; have a nice chat, write her a prescription.'"

Yisrultshe takes a pinch of snuff. With two fingers pressed together he signals to Gabriel, "Here, right next door. Soreh-Gitl had a respectable husband; he came from a prominent, well-to-do family. Go, Gabriel, go help. This is a holy thing, God's work. What you're doing, Gabriel, is easing people's suffering, even with a soothing word, with a bit of advice. When Jews are buffeted from all sides."

Ratse nods her cap in agreement. Tears trickle from her girlish eyes. "Go on, silly doctor. Go save a mother of children!"

9

SHMATTE REPAYS VOLF IN THE GRAVE

Bertshik Shmatte, Avreml "Treyf," and Oyzer, the small, anxious Smolin butcher, are standing in Butcher Shop Street, all mysteriously ruminative, till late in the evening, waiting for someone. Unable to wait any longer, Bertshik Shmatte loses his patience. He spits lengthily.

"To hell with the whole forequarter. To be kept standing all whole night for a lousy fifty groschens."

He slams the door forcefully, puts on his suede, fitted pants, smoothes out his close-cropped mustache, grabs the brass knuckles, which he never leaves his shop without, and sets off for Yisrultshe Blimeles'. The street is empty. He crosses that stretch safely. The brass knuckles haven't been necessary. Walking up the stairs, Bertshik recalls how when he was a child Tsvetl's father, Volf, used to rip his pants down and whip him right in the middle of the study house till he bled. Volf did it out of his own sense of pity for Bertshik. Everyone pitied him, mute

Khayim's son, the orphan; they all considered it a charitable act to teach him good manners with their fists. Now chamomile grows on Volf's grave, and Bertshik gets to kiss Tsvetl. And when he kisses her he experiences a double pleasure: both at the way his mustache brushes her smooth cheek, and at the vengeance he's taking on Volf. He waves the lamp about the dark hallway, fumbling for the door handle. Tsvetl comes out onto the stair. She puts a finger to Bertshik's lips. In the light of the electric lamp he sees Tsvetl's pale face. He follows her into the kitchen, sits down on a chair, takes out a handful of sunflower seeds, and scatters them onto Tsvetl's dress.

"Here, take 'em. I've sold three cartloads of bones. Tomorrow I'm going to the fair in Płock. What should I bring you, Tsvetl?"

He embraces her, soaking in her pale lips. Tsvetl runs out of breath.

"Leave me alone, Bertshik. You know very well how mother's heart's wearing out. The doctor was here today."

"The doctor in the linen suit? The one with the straw hat?" Bertshik laughs as his black eyes cut through the dark kitchen. "Listen, Tsvetl, you know I've loved you since we were kids. I always stared up at you when you lived over the pharmacy. But that father of yours, Tsvetl, I couldn't stand him. One's permitted to tell the truth about a dead man. Who could've imagined that today . . . Tsvetl, there's no woman more desirable than you. Just say the word, Tsvetlshi, whatever you want I'll do for you. I'm going to Płock for the fair."

The color returning to her face, Tsvetl stares deeply into Bertshik's eyes.

"Get a package to Moshke in prison." Her voice catches in her throat.

Bertshik, as if doused with cold water, indignantly lowers his hairy hands from her white neck. He stammers, impotent, through gritting teeth, "And how is that going to help, Tsvetlshi? One can achieve nothing by force. What can I say? If it were a matter theft . . . But Moshke, that snot-nosed brat, got his head all mixed up with politics. Anyway, I don't have any associates in his cell. Now come down here next to me, Tsvetl. My mother's gone off to help a woman in labor."

From the orchards come the sounds of sobbing. They pierce the night like a caterwaul. Then it changes to a whimper. Bertshik goes over to the window.

"Oho! Blind Khashe's not letting Grunem into her bed. You'll have better luck with me, Tsvetl. And stop knitting already! Take your eyes away from it."

Tsvetl sets aside the sweater and sits down next to Bertshik on the wooden bed. The door to the nook where Soreh-Gitl is sleeping is open. Tsvetl looks that way with damp, watchful eyes.

Bertshik's teeth are chattering. The electric lamp hardly glimmers. The mill beyond the city is panting heavily.

10

RATSE VISITS THE GRAVES
OF HER ANCESTORS

Not far from Hersh Lustik's orchard, to the side of the wide sandy path, the old Smolin cemetery stretches out along the Vistula, encircled by a half-sunken stone wall. In the early autumn, around the month of Elul,[13] people travel together to Smolin to visit the graves of their ancestors. Through the metallic rustle of leaves one could hear the sighs and sobs of women. Grunem stands guard over the cemetery. Seven times a day he would go back and forth with the keys, making moralistic admonitions for the sake of the foreign women visiting their ancestors' graves. They travel from the big cities, sporting hats and dressing fashionably so that the people of Smolin should see that they were no longer provincial women. But when they leave for the cemetery they remove their hats and coats and wrap themselves in old shawls; they lean against the crooked, moss-covered headstones and chatter at them in the same language and with the same God-fearing wrinkles on their faces as their mothers had once done. German settlers holding thick prayer books pass by on Sundays on their way to church. From the other side of the fence they would look those pretentious Jews over and decorously shake their brown, half-Slavic, half-Germanic faces: "*Die Juden beten zu ihren Vätern, schon nach der Ernte. Es stimmt genau.*"—"The Jews pray to their ancestors right after the harvest. That's exactly in keeping." And they would walk on, thinking of wicker baskets, of dried plums, of their settled economic life on the Vistula.

The forester of Smolin's woods, who usually drove the Jews off when they came out on the Sabbath for some fresh air, would leave them alone during the month of Elul. He would stand in the doorway of his forest hut in his broad, suede breeches, hunting gun slung over his shoulder, as he watched the Jewish cemetery, his face lashed by the wind. The woodcutters would sit by his door, eating whole-grain bread and brown *kishke*, listening to his stories with peasantly piety and alert ears.

"So I'm heading home from the forest with the wife. It's after midnight. The trees are rustling so mournfully it sounds like human souls crying on the wind. All of a sudden over by a headstone I see the timber merchant Yudke, the 'spy,' the one the Cossacks hanged when they returned from East Prussia. He's standing there, Yudke is, with his grey beard, wearing a black gabardine and tapping a little hammer against the headstone, carving out those angular Jewish letters. As soon as he sees me he grabs a stone and aims right for my head. 'Magda,' I say to my wife, 'are you seeing this?' 'I see it,' she says terrified and crosses herself. 'What do you see?' I ask as my teeth are chattering. 'The same thing you do,' she says, all pale."

The woodcutters burst out laughing and refill their pipes with tobacco. Under the forester's hostile gaze they recover their submissive demeanor, looking over disconcertedly at the Jewish cemetery and listening to the lamentations of the women.

At Hersh Lustik's orchard-hired workers are picking winter fruit. Hersh Lustik himself isn't there. He's off buying baskets from a German. Ratse is wandering among the trees, gathering the damaged apples that the pickers have left carelessly on the ground. She sorts them into several baskets. Autumn has diffused throughout the orchard. The grass, nursed by the sun, is bright green. Yellowish leaves cling bashfully to the colorful apples. A cool breeze blows up off the Vistula. In about two weeks' time Ratse would be leaving for town. Away from the open, fragrant orchard to the stifling little house with the cold sewing machine. They would be shut away in that house for the whole winter, waiting for the sun to be seen again in the yard and the cherries to blossom anew.

But Ratse is then reminded that she has withered, that for years she has stopped acting the way women do, that she has to haggle with Grunem for him to say Kaddish for her in a hundred and twenty years or so.—It all fills her soul with regret. But past that, it's now the month of Elul. Her heart twitches within her from a distant, hidden longing. She leaves the orchard and runs to her father's grave in the cemetery, falling to the damp grass and embracing the cold stone. She pours her heart out into the grave:

"Righteous father, sainted father, remember your daughter Soreh-Gitl! The poor thing is very ill. Illustrious father, may you intercede for all of us, may you advocate for our entire household, for Soreh-Gitl's children, the orphans, poor dears, who have no father. May Tsvetl get her betrothed. And may Moshke be let out of prison. Oh my lovely father, my clever father! I've got enemies for free. They envy our abundant crop of winter fruit. The new year's coming, father. Please hurry and intercede for Soreh-Gitl, that she should have bread for her poor orphans. And not forgetting my Hersh; people have a good opinion of him. He finds favor in their eyes. He is my honor, the crown upon my head. He brightens my home. He wipes the tears from my face and fills my innards with joy. Oh father! Kind, pious treasure, remember me with favor, may my tears not be in vain, oh merciful father. My I succeed for my . . . for Soreh-Gitl's children; my womb, father, is closed, closed for ever . . ."

She gets up from the green stone, drying her cried-out eyes. The wind lashes the chestnut leaves on the headstone. Ratse stands still, her hands wrung out and her head sunk on her chest. She stares at the green moss growing on her father's headstone. Her eyes grow misty. Soon the tears well up once more and she begins sobbing anew.

⁂

Hersh Lustik hurries home from Cyncymin to his orchard. A cool Elul breeze whispers through the branches of the poplars arrayed along the sandy roadside. Rows of storks crowd their way across. The fields, cut low, lie embarrassed in their nakedness. The waves on the Vistula rise sullen and angry. Hersh is seized by a longing for people. He walks on with a mountainous load of baskets on his shoulder, stepping nimbly. All of a sudden he remembers that a man mustn't race, that hurrying is a sin. It drives joy away and shortens one's life. And if a man were sad, then he oughtn't hurry either. A little sadness is always useful; it gives seasoning to joy. Reflecting more deeply on the couple of years that have just passed, he sees he has things to be sad about. He has had to provide for his entire family. To marry off their children, and *their* children. But he hasn't been worthy of an heir of his own, the issue from his own loins.

By the Gilevke, the stream that encircles the town, stand sad willows with drooping branches. The earth cools his feet. Pale, late-summer spider webs are carried on the air, winding round his beard, stroking his cheeks as if to comfort him: *Poor Hersh, don't be sad! Our Father Abraham was blessed with his first son at the age of a hundred.*

But needless to say, Hersh knows his thoughts are mocking him. Because Ratse, his wife, is a pious woman, but she is obviously not Mother Soreh and miracles do not happen in this day and age. His soul grows even more sorrowful. He feels a dampness in his eyes, and his lips quiver of their own accord.

"*Oh, Man . . . His origin is dust and his end is dust . . .*" [14]

He looks at the black tilled earth of Cyncymin, at the crows scavenging through the refuse with their beaks, at a withered tree standing all alone in the middle of the field, at the stone wall of the cemetery that could be seen from afar. His heart weeps within him. His voice grows louder as it carries tremblingly over the fields: "*Oh, do not cast me away in my old age . . .*" [15]

He walks over the sandy path. The mountain of baskets and his sixty-two years all weigh on his shoulders. The sodden sky oppresses his mood, and the air smells of damp leaves. He could already see his orchard beyond the little bridge. He stands there amazed, chiding himself, "What's going on with you, Hersh? Crying like a woman? Shame on you! What will people say? Hersh Lustik a crybaby. Clearly those Germans from Cyncymin have given me some bad luck."

He stops by a crucifix at the crossroads, takes out his red kerchief, wipes his eyes, and smoothes out his damp beard, all the while humming a tune. His eyes regain their impish sparkle as his song echoes across the field.

11

THE SAINT MICHAŁ FAIR

The next morning, at the Saint Michał Fair, Hersh Lustik enters the marketplace with a bargeful of plums. Smolin is glowing in the sun. The red tin roofs are a single flame. Indian summer has come in the middle of Elul. Hersh leaves Ratse with the plums while he wanders around the fair, his eyes scanning everywhere, sniffing the air. He's on the hunt for something. The peasants greet him with a warm *"Jak się macie"*—How d'ya do!—as if he were the prince of the Smolin fair.

German colonists arrive with crates of tomatoes and cauliflowers, two kinds of produce the Smolin Jews consider unkosher even though the rabbi has permitted their consumption, just as he has permitted others to eat meat from the hindmost parts from which the prohibited components had been removed. He himself, however, is content with a sweet little cucumber.

From the Wyszogród road arrive tall wagons full of fruit. Stretched out behind them come the smaller yellow-painted carts of the people from the Łowicz region. They are transporting tablecloths and colored kerchiefs of their own make. Among the wagons stand young Jewish women selling footwear, ready-mades, and trousers. Up beyond that is the poultry market. Lazar Kurnik is driving home a flock of geese. His wife, Fradl the poultrywoman,[16] pursues him with a continuous barrage of abuse: "Murderer! The ducks swimming on the Gilevke are diseased. You're gonna make the whole town's dishes unkosher."

Avreml "Treyf" is buying a couple of calves. Calves are dirt cheap. But it turns out the Jews have stopped eating veal. So Avreml looks pityingly at the calves he has purchased, and his heart melts with grief that he would have to sell the meat at a loss. No one pays much attention to Gabriel Priver. If someone saw him he would belittle him: *A doctor without a practice; a doctor who'll take a zloty for a visit; a doctor who'll take half a zloty; a doctor who'll even take nothing. A free doctor. How good of a doctor could he be?*

As in the good old days of the great fairs, Yisrultshe Blimeles is quite distracted. It's been some time since he had busied himself in the affairs of the world. But he couldn't just sit at home. So he goes hither and thither, bustling about the doorway of his stone house. He exchanges greetings with familiar Germans, offering them a pinch of snuff and inquiring about baskets and flax. People doff their Maciejówka caps to him and greet him with a *"stary Srul"*—Ole Srul.

Yisrultshe sees that the world is still the same old world, and that peasants are the same peasants who treat an old Jew with respect. Sixty years they've lived together in peace and friendship. Tall Maciek with the lively Adam's apple and the long, grey mustache bows to him: "*Panie* Srul, brought you a rooster for *kapores*, pure white, to pardon your sins. One zloty, *Panie* Srul."[17]

Yisrultshe offers Maciek some of his cheap tobacco. He then takes the rooster and blows apart the feathers covering its esophagus to examine it in the sun.

"A fat bird. So, Maciek, what're people talking about in the village?"

"Well, the winter sowing's about to start."

"But nothing bad, Macieju?"

Yisrultshe looks him deeply in the eyes, familiar, intimate.

"No, *Panie* Srul, nothing bad."

Yisrultshe Blimeles feels a weight has been lifted. He pays Maciek the zloty for the bird and takes it up to his place to see if Zisl's boil has finally burst.

Among the carts of notions sits the widow Soreh-Gitl, pale and speechless, next to a small table of dried woolens. Her heart feels weak, very weak. Her doctor had ordered her to get fresh air, so there she sits among the wagons, watching over the stall. Tsvetl is the saleswoman. Little Pesele, her sister, brings out the knitted gloves that Tsvetl had readied for the peasants for wintertime. Knitted wool sweaters, knit caps. In the distance, among the saddlers and rope-makers, stands Bertshik Shmatte with old metal goods. He doesn't take his eyes off Tsvetl's stall. If a brawl were to break out in the market he, Bertshik, would be ready with iron bars and brass knuckles.

Behind Bertshik, Grunem is clinging to a small sack of buckwheat. The festering wound on his foot is hurting more than ever. The pain radiates all the way up to his navel. Even though it's warm outside, Grunem doesn't know whether that was because he had just been going from village to village buying buckwheat or if it was due to fear and anxiety: *What if something should break out . . .*

Grunem knows he is putting his life in jeopardy going to the village. But that's how he proves his manhood. You can't be a man if you don't risk your life.

Khashe, Grunem's wife, doesn't engage in business. She walks all around the market with her watchful eye on the lookout for bargains. She goes with her children from stall to stall. She tastes a pear and has the children try a plum as she picks up a nearby apple. Khashe's children feel some welcome reprieve from their empty stomachs and sense that the fair has really come to Smolin.

Peasant wagons stand in front of Yosl Katazhan—the "Convict"'s—place. Katazhan's servants are filling warehouses with wheat. Chickens walk among the carts, pecking at the stones. Khashe is no worse than a chicken. She crawls under one of the wagons, sits down on the ground, spreads out her apron, and starts gathering kernels along with the chickens. Yosl Katazhan—an average-sized man with a black, Assyrian beard and greasy cheeks—gets angry at her: "Hey you, brood hen! Get outta there! You're chasing my chickens away. Go peck that father of yours, he's got a house."

Khashe sticks her head out from under the wagon. "Peck, peck. You should get a good pecking, ex-con! They're watching my father greedily. He's got it and doesn't want to give it to me. All my enemies should have what my father's got, apart from his heart condition."

An angry glint appears in Katazhan's eyes. "Bum! Pour out that wheat for the chickens or I'll have the custodian to take a broom to you. Janowe! Janowe!"

Ber Faytalovitsh arrives holding his silver walking stick. He walks with an airy step, his beard neatly combed, just as it was when he was still the great discounter. Everyone knows that Ber Faytalovitsh has funds frozen solid in his estate, that his daughter's dowry has been lost because of a moratorium. But Ber himself feigns ignorance and goes on acting in his aristocratic manner. He even wears low-cut chamois boots, and, out of noblesse oblige, doesn't get involved in Jewish communal affairs. Yosl Katazhan, despite being a newly influential person in Smolin, still feels insignificant next to Faytalovitsh and looks at him with respect. He lets Khashe go with her apron full of wheat. Her children run after her, clapping their little hands and raising a ruckus across the marketplace.

Ber casts Katazhan a long, mute look. He then takes his silver walking stick and sets off towards the sounds of a piano wafting, hoarse and chilly, from his open window out into the marketplace.

Gabriel wanders around like a fifth wheel. Here is Shmuel Loyvitsher's dry goods store. They have to treat him cordially here. It's his family after all. Gabriel's like a big child who wants everyone to coddle him. He looks for warmth everywhere. But

Sheva pushes the kerchief up on her head and scrunches up her nose, meaning: *that nuisance of a doctor.* She has no intention of entertaining guests right in the middle of the fair. Golde herself stands like an outsider to the conflict, her hair disheveled, arguing with a customer. She pretends not to notice Gabriel; she is aloof, heedless of his emotional state. Gabriel stands dazed in the middle of the marketplace not knowing what to do. Someone pulls him by the sleeve.

"Here, this way, Doctor Gabriel, to the left, behind the office. A foreign woman's gone into labor in the charity hostel."

Gabriel turns around. Hersh Lustik, looking artfully innocent, is heading off to his barge of plums.

12

YISRULTSHE BLIMELES STILL WANTS TO ENJOY A LITTLE NAKHES [18]

What's going to happen with Golde?

In Yisrultshe Blimeles' somnolent mind something is stirring. It's as irritating as Titus's flea.[19] "Yisrultshe!" he hears a voice from heaven. "Yisrultshe, you still have something to accomplish in this world. A nineteen-year-old grandchild. *Before new calamities befall the Jews, go snatch her away and make a marriage match*." He is overcome with a passion, a great desire to see Golde led under the marriage canopy. He feels that then he might feel some rejuvenation. So he torments his daughter:

"Sheva, that girl's all grown up. You're gonna commit a sin against God if you don't get her married!"

And to his son-in-law:

"Shmuel, the Jewish community's not going to run away with your chairmanship. Go and get Golde's head covered!"

Sheva lays a hand across her high bosom and tightens her lips.

"And what'm I in such a hurry for, papa? One of those ne'er-do-wells loafing around town?"

"Not one from around here; someone from abroad. Our Father Abraham also looked abroad. Better a foreigner, Sheva."

Shmuel Loyvitsher is chewing something sticky. His words come out with a glugging sound, like from a bottle.

"We know very well what's good, whether from here or from abroad. What stunning matches these days! Yosl Katazhan wanted to marry into a prominent family and he did so with one that wasn't local. And what did he get out of it? That son-in-law of his from Płock wanders around the marketplace, begging yer pardon, in those underwear what they call *pyjamas*. And that magnificent son-in-law cost him 5,000 zlotys. In my day, when one married off a child, y'either brought him into yer shop, or you set him up in a shop of his own. Nowadays all y'hear is: *Obtain for the groom a permit certificate to go to the Land of Israel . . . Endeavor to get a visa for Australia . . .* A student living off room and board, father-in-law, is not what I'm working so hard for! My children are growing up. I want to give Golde what she deserves—and there's an end to it."

Yisrultshe has a fit of sneezing.

"Woe to the ears that hear such things! Shmuel, it's possible to be both at the same time: a merchant and a learned person. You have to look for a match, Shmuel. Sitting around twiddling your thumbs waiting for a match to just appear is no plan. Golde's an obedient girl; for as long as she's young she'll do what her parents say. It's a different world today. Time was, parents made a match. A mother would say: 'Daughter, wash your hair, a potential groom's coming to see you today.' And a father would say to his son: 'Polish your boots, you've got a *viewing*.' Nowadays it's the opposite. Today a daughter says: 'Mama, put on a new wig, a potential groom's coming to see me. Papa, take off that tattered old gabardine . . . ' You mark my words so you won't regret it later. Before I depart this world I still want to enjoy a little *nakhes*!"

"No one's stopping you, papa. If you want to start looking around, go ahead," Sheva says with the outward nonchalance of someone used to asking.

It's not the easiest thing in the world for Yisrultshe Blimeles to go looking around for a match. His eyesight is weak and he couldn't hold a pen the way he used to. He has to resort to Oyzer the butcher and his ornate handwriting. Here, too, one has to be very careful in case the match came to nothing, then it'd be hush-hush.

The next morning, the Smolin postmaster takes out of his box five postcards written in Hebrew letters. All of them are addressed to rabbis and all of them bearing the same return address: *Yisrultshe Blimeles*. The postmaster is very surprised that in his old age Yisrultshe Blimeles has taken up correspondence in so many towns. Being no peasant, the postmaster thinks to himself: *Yisrultshe Blimeles is the oldest Jew in town; he knows what he's doing. The Jews are probably getting ready to leave Smolin. What the newspapers were saying a year ago is beginning to come true, and the Jews are starting in the town where he is postmaster. It's good—the Jews are leaving of their own accord; no one's forcing them. Tonight, at the reception for the pastor who had just returned from Germany, he would astonish the guests with this news.*

13

BECAUSE OF THE PASTOR, GABRIEL DISHONORS THE SABBATH TABLE

Gabriel devours one book after another. It's a welcome change of pace after the newspapers and radio programs. He wants to break free of his wire-bound captivity in favor of a quiet, soft green meadow. All the better to forget the day, to put reality out of his mind. Then he would be saved. He had made his diagnosis: the illness is contagious, but the poison was manufactured in special laboratories. From there it spreads across the country to infect more people. Now psychological therapy is necessary. The most important thing is for the patient not to think about his illness.

No patients at all come to him. Smolin doesn't hold medicine in high regard. Even though all of them suffer from one and the same disease. The contagious Jewish disease of self-torture and nightmare. The piano is stubbornly silent at Ber Faytalovitsh's. Nervous female footsteps could be heard through the thin wall.

At night the master of the house groans in his bed: "Mora . . . mora . . . moratorium . . ."

Ber Faytalovitsh is ill, so his daughter, Ruzhke, has to call Gabriel. But apparently she is going to wait for Gabriel to enter before making introductions.

Gabriel is incapable of imposing on people. Going to visit patients, though, is something different, and Ber Faytalovitsh, the Smolin discounter, is something else again. He closes his book, turns off the light, and walks out into Church Lane. Taking side streets he circles around the German church. The girandoles at the pastor's are burning festively. The tables are laden with bottles of red wine and trays of roasted fowl. The reception is in honor of the pastor's return from Germany. What news had he brought from Berlin? In Smolin it is being said in the pastor's name that in Germany Jews are once again living in peace and no one experiences any horrors.

The mayor, ruddy and cheerful, and altogether consoled after the death of his wife, is sitting at the head of the table. Next to him sits the postmaster, who is discussing something with him. The pastor's young wife is sitting with the priest on a separate couch, engrossed in a deep conversation. Side tables had been readied for bridge. The pastor—a tall man with dark hair and lively black eyes, and dressed in a long black jacket—circulates among his guests, uncorking bottles of wine and making sure their glasses are never empty. Eight groschens is what the pastor got from an acre of land, twenty zlotys for a wedding, thirty for a funeral. But the German colonists in Cyncymin are up in arms. The pastor is too rich: his own car, three trips to Berlin a year. And if Berlin, then what is he, Gabriel Priver, supposed to be doing at the pastor's? They all know he's a Jew. But they haven't invited Gabriel Priver the man but rather Gabriel Priver the doctor. Snobs! If it's a doctor they want to rub elbows with, then he could also be a Jew. No, he would decline the honor.

He turns round homeward. As he emerges into the marketplace, candles glimmer in the Jewish windows. He had completely forgotten that today is Friday. Because of the pastor who had returned from Berlin he had dishonored Yisrultshe Blimeles' table, the Friday-evening table that reminded him distantly of his parents' home.

It's already well after the meal. The doors open. Golde appears in a white blouse. Whom is she looking for in the marketplace? She walks in the direction of School Street. She has a girlfriend there, Baltshe, the rabbi's daughter. But Baltshe is probably sitting right now by the Sabbath candles in her father's study, reading Freud. Gabriel intercepts her.

"Good Sabbath, Golde."

A maternal kindliness radiates from Golde's white blouse. Her black hair is redolent of pine sap. Gabriel can feel the warmth of her breath. His hands, which had caressed countless women, are stricken lame by Golde's innocent smile.

They walk along the flour-dusted *chaussée*, a silver sheen on the rising moon.

"Come on, Golde, let's go to the mill. We'll take a rest on one of the stones."

He longs to tell her of his life and his wanderings. Undoubtedly she would understand him; Golde would naturally sympathize with him.

"Has my cousin already eaten?"

"Don't call me 'cousin,' Golde. Call me 'you'."

Golde is embarrassed.

"I can't. After all, my cousin is older."

She sits tall and straight on the stone. Her body has something of the lissomeness of the pines in Smolin's forest. Her movements are subdued, her eyes calm. The strain of life in the big city has left its traces on Gabriel's mood. His thoughts race, nervous and restless.

"I've always been a grown-up, Golde. Now I would just like to be a child, to recover myself for a while."

Golde regards him with gentle, motherly eyes.

"My cousin is always so meditative, and sad."

Gabriel strokes her hand.

"A great happiness has been rising in me, Golde, since I've been in Smolin. I'm recovering everything that I . . . Day by day I feel closer to people."

Sparks fly from the mill. The sound of carefree laughter wafts over the *chaussée*. Golde remains still.

"My girlfriends are waiting for me. Maybe even Baltshe."

Gabriel passes his hand over her hair.

"What does Baltshe do for you, Golde? And your girlfriends? Look how beautiful the night is. How fragrant the trees in the forest are."

Golde shrugs her shoulders.

"And what good does the forest do for people? I would much rather go to Warsaw. I'm sick of Smolin. I want to take classes."

"Golde, listen how the night birds call. The forester told me a silly story about demons who disguise themselves as night birds. I told him that the demons were not in the forest but only in the big cities. Golde, you must stay in Smolin. What use would Warsaw be to you? What use would classes be? The real work is accomplished quietly, apart. I have so much to tell you. Let's start our studies systematically. Golde, starting tomorrow, alright?"

The dew descends on the fields of Smolin like a barely visible dusting of snow. Golde's hair glistens. Her body shudders. Gabriel wraps her in his coat. His lips brush against her hair.

14

THE FREUDIENNE OF SMOLIN

The synagogue in Smolin is tucked away in a long yard, hidden from malicious eyes. The way one hides away a beautiful girl. She is neither dressed up nor adorned, so as not to arouse the desire of strangers. But here, at the end of the street, the open fields begin. Not right away. First there's a ditch. Next to the synagogue stands the rabbi's house. The Smolin rabbi doesn't need to worry about having a roof over his head. Still, the roof is full of holes, and in the autumn one has to put bowls out underneath the leaky ceiling. The Smolin rabbi doesn't have a lot of work, so he busies himself with the roof and with preparing his modern sermons so they'd be crowd-pleasers for his contemporary audience.

"Our rabbi," boast the people of Smolin, "is a wonderful human being! When he delivers a sermon it's a delicacy. He's a great expert. Speaks with equal ease of Maimonides and Lessing, Aristotle and Napoleon. An honest man. Lives in poverty and need."

The townsfolk consider this "poverty and need" his greatest virtue. The rabbi, however, sometimes does strange things that the town doesn't much find to their liking. What he did to his daughter they would never forgive.

The Gymnasium where Baltshe briefly studied, so they said in Smolin, was a Jewish one. The instructors wore fedoras and the girls prayed every day. But when a rabbi makes 40 zlotys a week in cash—the rest being taken on account as tax from the baker and the butcher—who is going to send his daughter to a Gymnasium. Baltshe has forgotten a lot of what she had learned there, but the townsfolk remember that the rabbi had tolerated that Gymnasium. And these modern mothers are angry at him that a pauper should disgrace the houses of the wealthy.

Baltshe herself bears her father a grudge. Those six classes were just a little something sweet, a teasing nibble to whet the appetite. She had been shown a path, a wide path into the big world, and in the middle of the path it turned right back round to Smolin. She *couldn't* associate with the other Gymnasium student girls in Warsaw, and with the Smolin girls she doesn't want to. Whether she actually doesn't want to associate with them is uncertain. It's possible she doesn't know how to talk to them. Baltshe spends her years in the women's section of the synagogue shut away in her books. It's not clear to Baltshe where her disinclination towards people comes from. From Freud she learned that she's suffering from a complex. But what kind of a complex? Where did her sufferings come from? The doctor, Gabriel Priver, might be able to shed some light on it, but Baltshe is too embarrassed to talk to him about it. He might suspect her of repressed things.

More than anything Baltshe is a shy girl. When speaking with someone she couldn't look them in the eye. She is ashamed of the freckles on her face and of the thoughts that she keeps hidden from people. She is ashamed that her father, the rabbi, secretly has to accept aid from the burghers of Smolin. She is ashamed that she still hasn't had any love affairs. She doesn't know how that happened. For her, the joys and sorrows of love are merely theoretical. If she weren't so ashamed she would talk a great deal! But Doctor Priver only listens to what Golde says, even though Golde doesn't know a tenth of what she, Baltshe, has already read. Baltshe withdraws into herself, digging deeper and deeper and uncovering more and more weaknesses, instincts, and traits that she inherited from both her father's and her mother's sides. Baltshe knows very precisely that her subconscious life is full of dark chasms and perils. That her character is warped. And as a result she could never be on familiar terms with people. The Smolin girls keep her at a distance because they think she's putting on airs. It's all the result of dreams she couldn't interpret for them. Some of the dreams cause her joy. If she had a good dream then the next day would also be a good one. Sometimes Baltshe dreams of conventional things: graduating from Gymnasium, studying psychology, healing people, smashing their complexes. She dreams that she has a friend, a great scholar who loves her passionately. Such thoughts cause a sweet warmth to suffuse her body. She enjoys it, but she's also ashamed because of her fantasies. So very ashamed . . .

When Baltshe is busy, though, she is a completely different person. Then she would give her little brothers something to eat, wash their under-*tallises*,[20] scrub the floors, and wait on her father who has shut himself in his office with the fifteen hundred notebooks for the books he is writing. It becomes clear to Baltshe that in his youth her father, the rabbi, experienced no erotic fulfillment. Now he's sublimating the sexual into the books he's writing.

Baltshe has no voice for singing. She can't paint. Nor does she have the imagination of a poetess. According to Freud, apparently she has a sickly imagination. Basically it comes down to the fact that she is the product of abnormal parents, even though they're called the Smolin rabbi and his wife. A whole town might have respect for the rabbi, but Baltshe knows the truth: her father is laden with inherited pathological traits. The nervous tic in his right eye, the strange hand gestures while reading, the grimaces and nose scratching. So many ugly traits she has inherited from her father. How many times has she tried to break her nail-biting habit! To no avail. Whenever she bites her nails she would stop herself, feeling that would finally be the last time. In five minutes, though, she would forget and start biting her nails all over again. Baltshe knows that without dealing with those trifling things she would never free herself from her complexes. Because of her personality she couldn't undertake serious work. Now there's still the matter of erotic excitement and the fantasies she experiences at night. After all, she, the rabbi's daughter, couldn't just go up to Bertshik Shmatte, the young man with the black eyes and the lovely mane of hair, and say "Come, satisfy me!" That might work for Tsvetl the knitter, for the girls from Butcher Shop Street who hung on Bertshik . . .

She picks up her mirror and examines herself closely: the freckles on her face, the high shoulders. Apart from her eyes, which are pleasant, she possesses nothing, nothing of the kind that might awaken a man's libido. No, she's an inferior creature, who doesn't know how to make the most of psychoanalysis. Every time she underwent treatment she just got all the more muddled and found new complexes within herself. There is one method, a radical one, to liberate oneself from one's complexes. But she would wait on that. She would give psychoanalysis one last try. If that doesn't help then she knows what she has to do.

15

HERSH LUSTIK BECOMES A MEMBER OF THE COMMUNITY COUNCIL

Whatever troubles Hersh Lustik endures from people, he still loves them and remains a good friend to them. But more than anything he loves being a free man. He'd never let himself be hitched to the cart: neither by worries, nor wife, nor petty desires, nor sweet morsels, nor flattering words, nor aggravations. But how could he be a free man when there are injustices in the world, when the common man is oppressed from all sides? The fine burghers do odious things while thinking themselves honest Jews entitled to the seats of honor.

So Hersh Lustik considers how he, a simple Jew, neither a wealthy man nor a scholar, could be helpful to people. He shies away from honors. He hates the community trough. But still, he has to do something so those on Cobbler Street might not die of want. So there he sits on Friday night by the brass candlesticks in his orderly little house, dunking challah in plum broth. On his lips is the tune to "Then was our mouth filled with laughter, and our tongue with singing."[21] The door opens and in come Lazar Kurnik, Bertshik Shmatte, and Avreml "Treyf." Behind them thrums a din and commotion from the Tailor-Farrier-Cobbler-Coachman Society—the entire Tailors' Synagogue.[22] Lazar Kurnik restrains the crowd shoving its way through the open doors. He chews the end of his ginger, straw-like beard. The visor of the round cloth cap perching right on the top of his head, which makes his face look rounder, is pushed snugly over his forehead. He folds his arms across his chest.

"Good Sabbath, Hersh! Haven't said grace after the meal yet?"

Hersh wipes his mustache and answers calmly, "Why the pretense: before the grace, after the grace? People say grace, they say grace. You're just after the gefilte fish. So, what good things are you gonna tell me on Friday night before the grace?"

Avreml "Treyf," dressed in his leather jacket with its whiff of the slaughterhouse, pushes his way forward to the table. Lazar the poultryman spreads his broad hands and stops the crowd.

"Don't push! Respect your elders. Hersh, it's no longer tolerable. Those good-for-nothings from the Hasidic prayer house, the muckety-mucks from the town, are going to take over the Jewish community. They're angry with the synagogue for praying on their own. Something's in the works. The drudges, you'll pardon me, are running around clearing the dust out of all of the offices, eating cakes with the powers that be and writing documents for us. And Yosl Katazhan has become a real big shot. Set his sights on being a council member. But *you* understand. Saying any more would be unnecessary. A wink'll do. So they want us, the poor common folk, to jam-pack the community tax. They'll get to remain respectable Jews while we'll be called the common herd. Hersh, we're not going to let ourselves be trampled under foot. We won't permit it. You—we're handing you the council membership."

Hersh Lustik's bushy eyebrows quiver. His pupils glimmer with a concealed fire. Whenever somebody wants something from him he treats it as if he were being guided by heaven. But

God is his witness that he doesn't do it out of vanity. He crosses one foot over the other and winks to his wife.

"So, Ratse, would you like to be a councilman's wife? My word, you've a right to treat yourself to a little honor once in a while too. Living so long with a man like me."

Ratse serves tea with their large Sabbath ladle. She's wearing a white starched apron and a red kerchief on her head. Her round, ever-worried eyes shine amiably. The Sabbath has washed away the dourness from her face. Her voice has lost its usual sound, and now it's warm.

"A councilman, is that so? Hersh the orchard keeper a councilman! Too splendid for me."

Lustik is in a cheerful mood. It could be detected in the smile concealed by his greying beard. He feels like making a bit of mischief with the crowd.

"Well, I've listened to the Tailor-Farrier-Cobbler-Coachman crew as well as you, Lazar. But the wife won't allow it. Mustn't go against one's wife. She koshers the meat, blesses the challah. If I gainsay her she'll go off on strike with the Lord Almighty. What'll I do then?"

Lazar Kurnik takes a step forward, his round cap again sitting on the edge of his forehead. His eyes wear a sternly demanding expression.

"Hersh, what do I need with your little jokes? They respect you, with their greasy bellies and fat, sanctimonious necks. City hall's going to remove the stalls from the marketplace, so the fairs will only take place on the Sabbath. We're supposed to see about doing something and you keep mum."

The crowd couldn't be held back at the door any longer. From all sides they jostle their way toward the table. Avreml "Treyf" gets snagged on the tablecloth, and the candlesticks and bowls of plum broth crash to the floor. Ratse cannot contain herself and starts hurling profane curses:

"Riff-raff, rabble, unwashed youths! Just look what the common herd'll do! Gone and taken the run of the place. Let me see the back of you on the other side of that door. Hersh, why are you saying *nothing*?! Don't you go getting your head all confused. That council membership'll blow up in your face and cause you nothing but grief. I don't want this town to be a curse in my old age. Let 'em make Yosl Katazhan a councilman. He's cut from a different cloth; he's got warehouses stuffed with grain. He . . ."

Hersh interrupts her, "Yosl Katazhan can't be councilman. He can't have the town hanging over his head."

"Why not?" Ratse asks angrily.

"Because Yosl Katazhan's got something else on his mind," answers Avreml "Treyf" from off to the side.

The crowd bursts into laughter. In the meantime, Bertshik has made his way forward. Bertshik Shmatte is dressed for the Sabbath in tall, polished boots. The same Bertshik who a year ago had busted Shmuel Loyvitsher in the sides because Shmuel had become head of the community. As a result, Bertshik was held for seven weeks in the prison in Płock. But it was worth it— he later bragged—it was worth it to teach a wealthy person a lesson. Now, however, he isn't speaking so boastfully. At home with Tsvetl, where Moshke's friends, the brush makers, gather, he has learned to speak gently and always about the oppressed poor man. So there he stands next to Hersh Lustik: Bertshik Shmatte—a tall, thin man with a hard, wind-beaten face, a carp's round, red eyes, and a blue shaven chin. He bangs his fist on the table, making the dishes crash once again.

"Hersh, those well-fed bellies are going to strike out our slate, the devil take their filthy hearts! Sucking the marrow from our bones and deceitfully leading people to believe we're not pious enough to be councilmen. They give themselves the choicest *aliyes* and stick us with the Torah lifting.[23] Packed stores. If the opportunity should arise, I swear I'd . . . We state explicitly in our program: the community shall open a soup kitchen, and also a library so the workers might be able to look through a book. Their taxes will finally be covered for once! And we're the ones to cover them. That's the program. You, Hersh, you're are a good person, one of us. You'll be in the first slot on our slate. We're going to rip open the bellies of those respectable Jews and let their guts spill out."

He stands by the cupboard, wiping the sweat from his forehead. Lazar Kurnik nervously chews on the tip of his straw-colored beard. The crowd loses its patience and starts making a commotion. Lazar raises a broad, hairy hand to quiet his people. Avreml "Treyf" bellows like an ox:

"Quite right, Bertshik, quite right! As I live and breathe, Hersh, they're gonna knock your windows out if you don't agree to be councilman. They're gonna shake the fruit from your trees. They're gonna get even with your wife somehow."

Hersh Lustik struggles his way through the crowd like a fish in a net.

"Listen, Ratse, they want you to dissuade your husband," he wipes off his beard. "Well, there it is; there's nothing for it. After all, if you've already come, it was probably my fate all along. Maybe some bit of salvation for the Jews will come of it, may it bring more justice to the world."

The crowd clears out into the marketplace under the starry sky, dragging Hersh along with them. He hums a cheerful tune to himself. Lazar Kurnik and Bertshik take up the melody and soon the whole crowd bursts into song:

> *Ein keloheinu—*
> *There's no God like our God.*

Avreml "Treyf" interrupts and bellows out:

> *Nodeh leloheinu—*
> *Let us praise our God.*[24]

They go from house to house, stopping under the windows of the wealthy and making the whole marketplace resound.

16

WHEN ONE WRITES A LOT,
THERE'S NOTHING TO COUNT

Early Sabbath morning the synagogue is chilly. The groggy crowd slurps their prayers like stale groats. It's hard to get warm after that Friday night. Meantime, there is no one present from the Hasidic bourgeois group. Since they had instituted a united Hasidic prayer house, going to the synagogue would be as bitter as salt in water. The walls had not been whitewashed, and the roof is full of holes. The fruit sellers and poultrymen who had wandered around the marketplace with Hersh Lustik till late into the night are shifting in their seats by the lecterns, yawning. The rabbi has only just arrived from the *mikveh*, his head still wet. He strides nimbly through the synagogue. Before they know it he is already standing in the corner by the ark, twisting his damp ear locks. Hersh Lustik sneaks into the synagogue from the side. Nevertheless, people notice him and bar his way from every side.

"Good Sabbath, Hersh! Good morning, Hersh!"

"Good morning, good morning. Now let me get over to the wall!" Hersh responds irritably, since the *"Borukh she-omar"* prayer is about to begin.[25] He throws on his *tallis* and tries to catch up with the cantor. The praying is now proceeding at too fast and buoyant a pace. People seem to be expecting something. Bertshik Shmatte stands by the door with his eighteen men, organizing them:

"If the rabbi talks about all of humanity and sides with the common folk—that's good. But if not, if he goes flattering the burghers, then . . ."

"Our synagogues," the rabbi begins his Sabbath sermon, as his *tallis* keeps slipping off his shoulders. "Our synagogues can be likened to the Holy Temple. When one doesn't cover the roof, God's house is ruined. You oughtn't think that because it's leaking in on my head that I'm rousing you to repentance. No, if it's leaking in God's house . . ."

Hersh Lustik listens to the rabbi's speech with eyes closed. His wide nostrils quiver. His forehead wrinkles.

"It's leaking in on my head," the rabbi sighs at the reader's desk, straightening his skullcap. "The councilmen keep going away, giving no thought to patching the roof . . ."

"It's leaking in on you, Rabbi? What does that mean? After all, don't you pray every day '*to hearken unto the tear-leaking and to the prayer*'?"[26]

The synagogue erupts into laughter. The rabbi smiles into his beard. Hersh Lustik had not shown him much respect, but he bears him no ill will either. He forgives him. With parables and the words of the sages, with biblical verses and maxims, the rabbi keeps returning to the same point—the roof. Bertshik Shmatte could no longer restrain himself. He makes his way closer to the reader's desk and bellows:

"But the councilmen *have* collected funds to repair the synagogue. Why have they forgotten the roof? Where's the bill? Why hasn't anyone written an account of how much was spent? You have to write it down, write it down. Before they leave, those respectable Jews, those thieves, let them write everything down. They sit at the Book and inscribe themselves for a good year."

Hersh Lustik shrugs his shoulders, "When one writes a lot, there's nothing to count . . ."

"Quite right, Hersh Lustik, he gave them a right talking-to," Shmuel Loyvitsher agrees. "The rascals! Become scribblers, they have. They should be taught bookkeeping."

They talk about rascals. But Bertshik cannot stand it. He stations his eighteen men on all four sides and himself walks up the steps to the ark, ready to give the command.

When the rabbi sees that Bertshik Shmatte and Avreml "Treyf"—Simeon and Levi[27]—are going to destroy the town he desires to make peace.

"Such blasphemy in a holy place! Calm your anger. That one of Israel should raise his hand against another? The hatred of brothers. *'Because of the shaft of a litter, Betar was destroyed,'* because of a . . ."[28]

Since Lazar Kurnik can see that the rabbi is clearly on the side of the respectable burghers he cannot keep silent.

"And invalidating slates, Rabbi? That's permissible? Seventy Jewish 'families' are still without a councilman. Denounced to the authorities. Said that we are such and such. Accused us falsely of going against the government. Is that just, Rabbi? To go along with informing and denunciation? Yosl Katazhan should be our spokesman."

"Justice? From a Cossack you demand justice?" yells Avreml "Treyf" as he thrusts his hands into the pockets of his weekday jacket as if steeling himself for something.

People are challenging the rabbi's probity and he pretends not to hear. He knows of no denunciations and has heard nothing of invalidated slates.

"If such has happened it's a loathsome thing. In the eyes of the Lord Almighty all Jews are equal, poor and rich, and *'even though Israel sinned',*"[29] he says, looking intentionally toward Avreml.

The crowd starts taking too much liberty speaking against the rabbi. That nettles Hersh. He stands up and bangs on the reader's desk.

"What's the use, Rabbi, of so much talking? Why do you need to make excuses? You there, roosters!" he yells at Bertshik's men. "Go home to your wives!" He drives the crowd out by their coattails.

Hiding behind the ark, Grunem's eldest son, Shloymele, lets out a long *cock-a-doodle-doo*, which leads to a stampede over the benches and lecterns. Old women from Synagogue Lane appear on the other side of the windows and taunt them in Russian: *Asho kuri do komuri!*—"Look at all the chickens in the henhouse!"

"Some service today. You may say the *Aleinu* now.[30] Hurry up and finish your prayers, and then go on home; all too soon the price of bread could go up."

Hersh Lustik tucks his *tallis* under his arm and leaves the synagogue for home. On the way, Yisrultshe Blimeles catches up with him. His forehead is as yellow as wax. He fixes his intense gaze on Hersh.

"A great trait, this sort of happiness, this general cheerfulness. Hersh, you are a simple Jew, but as much a peacemaker as Aaron the Priest. More so. Because you do it with joy."

17

HERSH LUSTIK GOES TO MAKE THE WORLD A BETTER PLACE

For as far back as the Smoliners could recall, Hersh Lustik was never able to tolerate injustice. Especially now that he's a councilman, he feels double the responsibility. People are constantly beating down his door. Whoever is aggrieved comes crying to Hersh Lustik. All of Cobbler Street carries themselves off to his orchard. It's as if they are flogging him with whips:

"Hersh, the world's behaving without a shred of conscience."

"Hersh, why is it my girl's gotta take up a position in service?"

"Hersh, my father-in-law Yisrultshe Blimeles' place has empty apartments while me and my six children have to live in one room."

"Hersh, have you ever heard of such a thing: the rabbi of a Jewish community eating bread and radishes as a meal?"

"Hersh, Hersh . . ."

Hersh Lustik grabs his head, "My dear people, stop Hershing me. Hersh this and Hersh that. Always Hersh! And what about

God Almighty? So many troubles (no Evil Eye) have accumulated in the world. You can't make them better all at once."

"But Hersh, where does so much evil come from?"

"What does it matter where from? As long as, thank God, there's . . ."

He picks up his long crooked walking stick, leaves the orchard to Ratse's care, and sets off into town to see with his own eyes all of the evil. Lazar Kurnik—who hadn't gone to Warsaw on account of a shattered wagon and is now supplying chickens to pious Jews who only eat poultry—keeps up with Hersh step for step, all the while whispering something in his ear. Bertshik Shmatte is too embarrassed to lift his eyes. Hersh Lustik knows it's because of Tsvetl, Soreh-Gitl's daughter, with whom Bertshik is having a romance, and not in the Jewish manner. Meanwhile, Bertshik is himself beset with big problems. People no longer want him selling his rags in the village and he has had to stop being a peddler. Avreml "Treyf" in his white apron joins up with them mid-way, the letter writer Itshe Tshap trailing behind.

They walk across the marketplace, their heads held high and casting haughty glances: *Our councilman!* They turn off down Synagogue Street and arrive at the councilman's office to a great commotion.

There behind the large table with the green tablecloth, under the portrait of Berek Joselewicz riding his white horse,[31] sits Shmuel Loyvitsher, the head of the Smolin Jewish community, munching on candy. Shmuel Loyvitsher blanches at the sight of the rabble. He rises, walks over to the cashbox, and turns the key in the lock, casting a sidelong glance at Hersh Lustik. He couldn't see the rest of the crowd.

"What good news have you come to tell me, Hersh?"

Hersh calmly smoothes his grizzled beard.

"We have come to you, Shmuel, in search of supplies. A couple of cartloads of peat, a cord of firewood, twenty or so bushels of potatoes. Winter's coming. Children are swollen with hunger. Houses are unheated. The Jewish community, Shmuel, is obligated . . ."

"But Hersh, you seem to be speaking with some authority, like a wealthy man. The community is not obliged to support a city with kindling," Shmuel Loyvitsher says, offended.

Hersh Lustik's mischievous eyes wander over the iron cash-box. His nostrils quiver.

"Seems you've become aware of my being a wealthy man, Shmuel, like a blind horse into a pit. So, what d'you have to say about it?" Hersh says, spinning round towards his men. "Hersh Lustik a wealthy man, eh? A wealthy Jew with groschens few."

Shmuel Loyvitsher straightens his glossy skullcap and leans comfortably against the arm of his chair.

"Your influence at home does not extend here, so temper your words. You'll achieve nothing by force."

"Shmuel, there are various powers in the world. Just as Rothschild is powerful in wealth, I am powerful in poverty. Am I a councilman or am I not? If, in turn, I *am* a councilman, then I get to have some control over the community's funds. Enjoy clutching that key there, Shmuel, just let me distribute . . ."

Avreml "Treyf" is gritting his teeth. All of a sudden he lurches forward like an ox ready to trample and gore the head of the community.

"People!" he bellows. "I can't stand it anymore. He's insulting our councilman!"

Bertshik Shmatte couldn't keep still either. All at once he feels Avreml is trying to beat him to the punch and wants to seize the initiative from him. So he pushes him off.

"Shove off and shut your yap. You've gotta know how to talk to these respectable Jews. Let me. Shmuel, I want to know if you're just pretending to be a fool or if you really are a lunkhead?"

Galled by this, Shmuel jumps up from his armchair. His soft, ruddy cheeks have gone pale. He bangs his fist on the table, which makes the little bell on the green tablecloth chime.

"I will not speak with you, you insolent man. You're a peddler, a criminal person. *Szmaciarz*, ragman, bone-picker . . ."

Bertshik Shmatte grabs his belt.

"Shmuel, I hope you meet a drunken peasant with a bagful of bones and he takes yours with him."

Hersh Lustik pushes Bertshik aside.

"Hush up, quiet! What good's all this hullabaloo? Shmuel, don't take it to heart. Better to mouth than to heart. You think that's what they're really saying? What they're expressing is the pain of the common people. Shmuel, write out a receipt to the forester for some wood. As for the potatoes, we'll be able to find a solution to that."

"Oh? The nerve of it! What effrontery to come storming into the community offices with all this riff-raff!"—Shmuel is still having a hard time getting over it.—"Here's your receipt for kindling and may my eyes never see these people ever again."

"You'll yet see something else with your eyes," Bertshik says, shaking his fist threateningly.

"Empty prattle. Action speaks louder than words!" Hersh holds the receipt up to Bertshik's mouth. "Just so, Shmuel. *Hakesef yayne es hakl*—Money oppresseth all.[32] You've done me a good turn, so may God reward you for your soft heart and let us not be enemies. After all, you're not from Błonie." [33]

In the courtyard Hersh Lustik turns towards his people and spits three times on the piece of paper.

"Well then, at least it's a start. By grueling effort I've gotten to be a councilman. Now we're going to see Yisrultshe Blimeles. Khashe with her blind eye, the poor thing, is living in a single room. Yisrultshe is her father. He owns a house, and Grunem, with all his hardships and suffering, is still his son-in-law."

"First to the priest about the fairs. We'll convince him to cancel the order!" urges Lazar Kurnik.

"While we're at it let's also talk to him about the slaughtering," said Avreml "Treyf," tugging on Hersh Lustik's sleeve.

"No!" Hersh Lustik says, unyielding. "Let's not worry about the priest. I'll speak with him in private. Nowadays you have to be careful. There's but a hair's breadth between loving Jews and hating them. Come, let's go see Yisrultshe Blimeles."

18

ONE LESS INJUSTICE

Yisrultshe Blimeles is sitting at the table, cutting slices of stale challah with the Sabbath knife. His long, bony fingers are trembling so he can hardly reach the wooden saltcellars. The eighty-three-year-old Zisl, with the tall wig braided like a challah, shuffles quietly across the room, all the while pouring coffee for her husband.

"Here, Yisrultshe, take a little butter, spread it on the challah. Otherwise, the challah will stick in your throat."

Yisrultshe's ashen, rheumy eyes watch eerily. He brushes the green flecks of tobacco off his grey beard.

"Butt'r, really? Enough butt'ring! The bailiffs don't pay rent. Town hall's ordered the house to be refurbished and a new side-walk put in. And you're talkin' butt'r! Butt'r . . ."

He opens a drawer and spreads out over the table invoices from the yeshivas, receipt slips from the alms fund, and, from the Jerusalem community, contracts for land in Palestine. He brings a yellow receipt with a large heading up to his eyes. Seized by a sudden long fit of coughing, his words come out in a drawl, rattling with phlegm.

"Just look, Zisl, it's clearly signed: *Zishe Gottesman*. Who could have expected that? Such an honest young man. Would've spared no effort. Eh, Zisl, why so quiet? Something's going to come of those twenty *dunams* of land?" [34]

Zisl groans.

"And what can I say, when people have to hide the disgrace. I've been telling you for quite a while that you should quit this business. I never liked him, that Zishe Gottesman. He was a schoolteacher in Sorczew. Now he's a real big-shot in the 'Agudah.' That's what happens when you don't listen to your wife."

A head appears in the gap of the open door. A pair of mischievous eyes come to rest on the portraits of the Kovner Rabbi and the Magid of Kozhenits. Yisrultshe's face brightens.

"Look who's here! Welcome, Hersh! From you we'll finally hear a comforting word. That business with the slaughtering's not going well, eh?"

"What, you don't eat meat, Yisrultshe? Well, you do only live on some groats and a couple of old loaves of challah from one Sabbath to the next."

"True, true!" Yisrultshe moans. "This body of mine takes no meat. But there are young men in the world who are nourished on meat. How many Jews—Lord help us!—will be thus *reduced to a loaf of bread*." [35]

Hersh Lustik shakes his head sympathetically.

"You're a compassionate person, Yisrultshe. If Smolin had ten more Jews like you I'd try to change the whole world. We've come to see you, Yisrultshe, on account of Grunem, your son-in-law. It would be an act of fairness if you'd give him some place or other in your house to live. Khashe is, after all, your own flesh-and-blood. As it is written: *As a father pitieth his children*." [36]

The food sticks in Yisrultshe's throat. He knocks over his cup of coffee, his rheumy eyes burning red with fire.

"What?! Give a whole new dowry for my daughter? Hasn't she drained me enough? Twice I set her up with a shop. Gave them an apartment, which they then sold. The profligates. They eat fresh rolls. If you don't have enough for beer, then drink water. I've got no apartments."

Zisl breaks a piece of coal by the kitchen, and stretches out a sooty hand toward Hersh Lustik.

"Such a good-for-nothing, that Khashe. Loading the old folks' shoulders with burdens. What does she think, that daughter of ours, that her father's a milk cow? She's gotten her apartments, the slattern."

Yisrultshe fixes his glazed eyes:

"It's a matter of *your eye shall not look with pity*.[37] One is not permitted to pity one's children, because when one pities children one becomes their enemy. As the Talmud states . . ."

Hersh Lustik interrupts him, "Yisrultshe, what's the good of all these things? *'The Talmud states'*; *'Rashi says'*; *'as it is written.'* The best thing is the midrash. When it's *'The midrash says,'* at least then you know you've got something. Even a little room has its role to play in such a stone building."

A smile plays across Yisrultshe's sour face.

"You're starting in with your jokes, Hersh. Grunem's a father, let him find bread for his children. Smoking cigarettes, sitting in the study house, talking politics as if he were one of the burghers. That'd be all well and good if the children were married off. His world's about to change. I've got no apartments."

"Yisrultshe, your grandchildren are cold in their room at night. Your daughter does the laundry with one good eye. Shloymele's schooling needs to be provided for. He's fallen into some bad habits."

Lazar Kurnik arrives with Bertshik. Hersh Lustik turns toward them.

"Were you there?"

"We were."

"Did you see?"

"We did."

"Is it like they said?"

"It's like they said."

"A house with a stove?"

"A house with a stove."

"Vacant?"

"Vacant."

"So, there's a house! Well, well, Yisrultshe. *There is no pride in Jacob.* One gets no pride from children. But without children, Yisrultshe, it's worse. Give some thought to the apartment for your daughter, Yisrultshe. It's a matter of *none did compel*;[38] no one's forcing you. Best of luck to you!"

No sooner has the door closed behind Hersh Lustik than Zisl stokes the fire anew.

"So, you've finally experienced an evil visitation! And meantime the coffee's gone cold. She's ruining our lives, that daughter of yours."

Yisrultshe considers a meager slice of bread.

"I'd be happy to give in to them, Zisl. My heart's endured enough pain. In any case, you can't take it with you into the grave."

⁘

A fat, round moon rolls its way into the Smolin marketplace, sniffing round the cramped yards. It slips calmly from one lane to another, accompanied by a pack of dogs that raises a howl over the town. Yisrultshe Blimeles tosses and turns on his bed. He cannot get to sleep. The light is stinging his eyes. He is tormented by queer thoughts. Hitler riding into Smolin on a black horse. Arabs stabbing Jews and befouling the Western Wall. He hears strange voices, distant footsteps.

"It's starting at last," Yisrultshe thinks and buries his head in his pillow.

In the marketplace windows open. Groggy heads appear. There is a big commotion in Yisrultshe Blimeles' yard. Grunem is sitting on a cartload of bedding with Khashe with the blind eye next to him, wrapped in a shawl. The sleepy heads of little children sticking out from among the pillows. Bertshik Shmatte,

Itshe Tshap, and Lazar Kurnik are wrangling with Yisrultshe Blimeles' watchman. Meanwhile, Avreml "Treyf" has come running up, undoing the clamps from the doors and passing the sleeping children through the window into the empty room. Hersh Lustik stands in the entryway rubbing his hands.

"One less injustice in the world."

Yisrultshe Blimeles is startled awake. He runs to the window in his wide under-*tallis* and stares down into the dark yard. He sees nothing. But hearing the crying of the children he understands everything. Slowly, groping his way along the walls, he gets back into bed, wraps himself up in the bedclothes, and, half-asleep, moves his lips, "A good man, that Hersh Lustik; he's lifted a weight from my heart."

19

HITLER DOES NOT BEAT PIOUS JEWS

Hersh Lustik rises at dawn and picks the last fruit from the trees. He bungs the barrels of plums and lays the apples in a bedding of hay. It's slippery in the orchard. Runnels of water stand in the hollows and a white frost has settled on the trees. Dressed in a quilted kaftan, Ratse gathers the domestic gear that lies scattered around the orchard. She zealously scours the pots; binds together the pipes of the iron stove; makes a bundle of the bedding; and sweeps the area around the wagon, as if it were a house that had to be cleaned when someone moved out. No trash must be left. She scratches the thin hair under her kerchief.

"*Brrrr*. Foul weather."

Hersh spreads his hands and rubs them over his arms to warm them up.

"Oh no, Ratse, don't go on about the weather. All of life is nothing more than some sun and some rain. A caress, a burn . . ."

The German Witbrot makes his way across the orchard, his pipe in his mouth. His heavy, beer-soaked eyes range happily over his well-established property. His clipped words have an acerbic tone.

"Please to tidy ze place up, *Frau* Lustik; *Ordnung* zere must be. Haf you had a goot year, Hersh? Ze garten has served you well, *nicht wahr?*"

"I can't complain, *Panie* Witbrot. A good crop, a not-so-good crop. What more is there to say?" Hersh answers and returns to what he was doing.

Witbrot doesn't take the pipe out of his mouth. His fat, resonant voice is hoarse: "You are keeping silent. Goot, *Panie* Lustik. A clever silence. But *challah, bosor ve-dogim* shall you eat every *Sabbat.*" [39]

A proud sparkle appears in Hersh Lustik's eyes.

"That's why we're Jews, after all, *Panie* Gerrrman, so we can eat challah."

"*Ja, ja, Juden*, Gott's chosen people. In Deutschland you eat pork; in Chicago you work on ze *Sabbat*. A very large city, Chicago. Sree sousand oxen zey slaughter every day. I haf traveled much, *Herr* Lustik. Haf been to Canada. To Liverpool. To Moscow. Before ze war. Fortyfold forty bells. Sree times to Berlin. Brought my Dobermann from Deutschland. A clever dog, *nicht wahr?* From a noble breed. Come here, Dobermann. *Frau* Lustik, giff him no more cholent. It is not goot for him."

Dobermann, a tall, black dog, with smooth skin and old, watery eyes sullenly approaches Ratse's pots and starts licking them, systematically and thoroughly. Hersh winks to his wife.

"Ratse, take those pots away. No need to make trouble. The dog has a delicate stomach."

"*Ja*, ze dog is from Deutschland," Witbrot says, his eyes brightening. "Deutschland, Deutschland! What a beautiful country. Great inventions zey haf in Deutschland. Deas rays zat can stop ships and trains. Deutschland, you know, gets everysing back. Ze Jews are to blame zat we lost ze war. A lovely book, ze Old Testament. Zat Moses was a godly man. But ze fact zat he spoke so closely wis ze Goot Lord, face to face, zat cannot be conceived. Zis Hitler, you know, does not beat pious Jews. He beats communists. Cleanse ze place, *Frau* Lustik . . ."

"Yes, yes," Hersh says, arranging the baskets of apples in a row. "He is thinking of the communists. But the blows fall all the same on the Jews."

Witbrot pretends not to hear. He signals to Dobermann and walks over to the dovecote, taking a handful of barley and scattering it for the doves.

Lazar Kurnik arrives with a wagon half-full of poultry. The orchard is overwhelmed with the quacking of ducks and the honking of geese. Kurnik starts loading the fruit, arranging the barrels of plums in the empty half of the wagon. Red beaks peck at the barrels. The young roosters crow, enlivening the autumn morning. Ratse loads the domestic gear and bedding onto the wagon, sits down on top of the featherbeds, and shouts down to the German, "Goodbaaa, *Panie* Witbrot."

Witbrot, dressed in yellow trousers, comes out in front of the door with his wife, the diminutive German woman with the tall bun on her head. Behind them stand the children of their unmarried daughter Berta, their half-Slavic, half-Germanic faces buried in the wide folds of the German woman's dress. And Dobermann is there, too. He's walking round the wagon on feeble legs, sniffing the wheels. The whole household watches with longing eyes as the orchard keeper and the orchard keeper's wife leave the orchard. Witbrot calls out after them with his hoarse voice:

> *Leben Sie wohl, essen Sie Kohl,*
> *Trinken Sie Bier, denken Sie auch an mir.*

> Farewell! Eat cabbage, drink beer,
> Remember me with good cheer.

20

FOR THE LITTLE
CHILDREN'S SAKE

Winds lash Smolin from all sides. Streams overflow, turning the roads into a swamp. Houses with smoking chimneys lie hobbled like goats in the mud. Brush makers in their garrets stand around in their jackets cleaning boar bristles for the new season. Anyone who had thought to fit out a room with turf in advance is now warm. In Cobbler Street little children are freezing. In the schools, boys sit in front of their Talmuds, shivering. Illnesses make their rounds of the town. Old women from the synagogue run from place to place with bottles of alcohol. Itte the midwife, Bertshik's mother, assists them. She rubs liniment on children's little bellies and wards off the Evil Eye. The smell of phenol diffuses across the courtyards. The little bit of wood that the community had distributed has long been reduced to ash. At Grunem's, the children eat only frozen potatoes and lie for days in bed, waiting for the hunger to pass. But it doesn't pass. Khashe keeps running to her stepmother, Zisl, for help. Hersh Lustik comes to understand that he couldn't rely on the community itself, that these days the council is a weak form of support. One has to get things done on one's own, by one's own effort.

Severe frosts have set in. Important people have come from Warsaw with hunting dogs and with guns slung over their arms. An honored guest accompanies them: a government minister from Prussia. The pastor, the priest, and the pharmacist join the hunting trip. People press Hersh Lustik: "It's dangerous to go into the forest for wood."

Hersh Lustik laughs, "You don't flee the Lord Almighty. Whoever's fate it is, the bullet hits his house."

That morning he heads off into the wood. With a bag over his shoulder and a rope around his hips. A frosty bedding of snow lies under his feet, emboldening him. It's not for his own good that he's risking his life. He's going for the sake of the poor people. He considers himself their representative.

He emerges onto the Cyncymin road and walks along the orchard. By Witbrot's yard the smell of freshly brewed coffee tickles his nose. Inside the German's house, behind the windows with the blue curtains, it's cozy and warm. Hersh looks out across Witbrot's estate. Near the barn lie a couple of cords of wood that Witbrot has readied for winter. The potato troughs have been covered with straw. The well is sealed up. "Provident people, these Germans!" Hersh Lustik thinks. "They get everything in order, dependably and in good time. The Prussian minister will be quite satisfied that his countrymen are living so well in our domains."

He comes out into the orchard. The straw hut lies stretched out like a flayed horse. Only the naked ribs—its white staves—are visible. The rains have wrought a massacre in the orchard. The plum trees stand crooked, their still living branches broken off. Their bark is flayed, revealing their naked bodies. He is overcome with pity for these trees, their lives cut short, and for the fruit sellers who would suffer a bad year as a result. He feels something licking his knee. He turns around. There is Dobermann.

The tall dog with the smooth coat and watery eyes is nuzzling him. Hersh Lustik is startled.

"That really you, Dobermann? A German dog messing about with an old Jew. What'll your master say?"

Dobermann lowers his tail and barks woefully towards Witbrot's house. He actually feels guilty. His eyes display the meekness of a dog beaten regularly. Hersh Lustik's heart goes out to him. He caresses Dobermann, petting his back, his neck, when suddenly Dobermann jumps up. His short hair stands on end, turning stiff and prickly. He opens a mouth full of old, rotten teeth, ready to tear him apart. Hersh notices an open wound on Dobermann's head. The skin is flayed down to the skull and the blood hasn't completely congealed. Hersh stands as if stricken lame, not taking his eyes off the dog. Both are silent. Dog and man understanding one another through their eyes.

"Poor Dobermann! How the pastor's hunting dogs have abused you. But they're German dogs, too, after all. Blood of your blood and flesh of your flesh. Come on, Dobermann, off to your master, let him heal you!"

Witbrot conceals the warmth of his home from strangers. Hersh Lustik knocks on the nail-studded door. It takes a long time for the German to appear. He stands in the doorway, wearing a yellow jacket, his pipe in his mouth. In his hand a calf's foot with leather straps. Sobbing could be heard inside. It is his unmarried daughter, Berta, crying. Her children, beaten, are locked in the cold barn. Witbrot stands there, furious. His eyes alight with blood. Spying Dobermann, he shouts at the dog with his smoky voice:

"*Mache, Dobermann, daß du fortkommen sollst.*—Make sure you scram, Dobermann. Roaming around vis ze hunting dogs like some young bitch. Drop dead!"

Dobermann limps slowly away from Witbrot's feet. But he doesn't get to the doghouse. Halfway there he stops, as if he has suddenly reconsidered, and stretches himself out to his full length. Even from a distance one could see the wound on his head turning red, standing out against the whiteness of the snow. Witbrot wants to go to the dog. The little German woman with the tall bun appears and grabs her husband's arm.

"*Schneller, Fritz; die Magd stirbt. Sie hat Stürzwehen.*—Quickly, Fritz; the girl's dying. She's having labor pains."

Hersh Lustik casts a sidelong look at Dobermann, sighs, and continues on his way.

In the forest, the conifers are green. Little pools, covered with thin films of ice, glitter amongst the trees. White gobs of snow stick in the crannies of the tree bark. The forest is empty, windblown. The distant crack of hunting guns, resounding in a thousand echoes. Through the sparse trees comes a cold and frosty barking. Hersh Lustik's eyes are momentarily dazzled: a small grey hare with a lame foot comes pounding through the woods heading toward the Jewish cemetery. There it would disappear among the densely overgrown headstones. Hersh walks along the well-worn path till he comes to the forester's hut.

The forester, his gun slung over his shoulder, is dressed in a green, military-style uniform. In a large heath, enclosed by plaited fencing, young does and stags with braided antlers caper about. They goggle their eyes at Lustik, sniffing him with moist snouts. The forester takes a cigarette from his tobacco pouch. He spits brusquely.

"Hershek, cur's blood. Not afraid to come into the forest, eh? People are shooting, Hershek. Now here's an intrepid Jew."

Hersh takes the bag from his shoulder and unties the rope from his hips.

"What do I have to be afraid of, *Panie* Forester? After all, they're not hunting Jews. They're shooting hares."

The forester bursts out laughing loudly, like a nobleman.

"If they needed to, they'd shoot Jews too."

"But in the meantime they obviously don't need to."

"What have you come for, Hershek?"

"For a few dried branches for some poor people. Children are freezing."

The forester rubs his stiff brow.

"I've got no wood for the likes of you. You really must have sinned, you Jews. Dark days are upon you. But come now, Hershek, tell me, where is it that they actually like Jews? Dammit! Because of you yids I can't sleep. Every night they come to me in my dreams. Most of the time it's that one with the ear locks, Yudke the timber merchant, the one the Cossacks hanged in front of my window. You understand? The hell with it, a person's allowed to make a mistake once in a while! It just seemed to me they were spies. As soon as it's midnight they crawl out of their graves and come right into my hut. They want to strangle me, the devils. Take your wood, Hershek, however much you want. What are they saying in Smolin about Danzig?[40] Jews always know everything in advance. Is there going to be war, Hershek?"

Lustik breaks down the branches and gathers them into bundles. Busy with the work he's not listening to the forester who becomes angry.

"Why are you silent, Hershek?"

"Eh?" Lustik replies like someone hard of hearing. "I've said nothing and I've insulted no one."

The forester's temper flares.

"I'm asking you, Hershek, if there's going to be war. The Germans want to seize Danzig."

"Danzig? How would I know? For a Jew, *Panie* Forester, the less spoken the better. If it's destined to be, then there'll be war as well. Whatever's deserved. *Panie*, give me some dried mushrooms for a poor Jewess. And maybe some rose honey? I'm going to set some aside for wine for the Sabbath."

The voices of people could be heard in the distance, drowned out by the barking of dogs. Priestly cloaks flutter among the trees. Hunting guns stand out above the wide, black hats. Hersh Lustik grabs his basket of mushrooms and sighs.

The forester casts him a menacing look and catches him firmly by the arm.

"Why are you sighing, Hershek?"

"I'm sighing, *Panie* Forester, because I'm thinking of the Smolin rabbi who sits for months at a time shut away in his study, content with his daily piece of bread and some stale groats. *Panie*, have you ever once seen the rabbi go hunting?"

He heaves the bundle of wood up onto his shoulder, shaking his head.

"*Bóg zapłać!*—May God repay you well!"

And he leaves the forest before the hunters arrive.

21

SOREH-GITL FEARS FOR A RING

A pale Sabbath evening descends over Smolin. The orchard courtyard is swathed in white. The snow on the rooftops sparkles with violet light. The gloom of a short-winded day expires longingly as it drifts among the little wooden houses. Lazar Kurnik's cart is covered in snow as if packed with cotton. It stands with its wagon shaft pushed up toward the rising stars. Avreml "Treyf"'s ample koshering board sprawls next to the wagon. The moon illuminates them both. The board and the cart are having a discussion:

"Me and all the goods got overturned at the Boża Wola fair. Broke my ribs."

"And they're not going to kosher meat on me anymore," the board groans.

The scent of Antonówka apples wafts down from the attic—the fruit that Hersh Lustik had bedded in straw.

"We've got nothing to worry about. Every summer we'll bloom anew in the German Witbrot's orchard."

Ratse stands at the window, looking up at the pale stars. She puts her fingers to the windowpane, wetting them in the frost as she recites "God of Abraham." [41] Ratse's sister Soreh-Gitl is sitting by the sideboard, wrapped in a Turkish shawl like a widow in her mourning dress.

"Oh, how we've talked ourselves out!" Ratse says. "What a starry sky. Time to light a candle."

Soreh-Gitl catches her sister by the hand, "Just wait a little, Ratse. Why are you in such a hurry? Saturday evenings, after the Sabbath, I like to sit in the dark. That's when it feels as if the whole world is grieving with me. You must realize, Ratse, that it's already been nearly a year since Volf's death. Every Friday evening he comes to me in my dreams."

Ratse's grey, baleful eyes mingle with the darkness suffusing the room.

"I don't know why he torments you so, that husband of yours. What does Volf want from you?"

Soreh-Gitl purses her little mouth.

"Nothing. Always the same thing. The children, only the children. Toiled his whole life for the sake of the children. I'm supposed to see to setting some goal for them. But go set goals for children these days! Now that he's left me a miserable widow."

Ratse breathes heavily. The apron rises over her belly.

"I have to tell you the honest truth, Soreh-Gitl. He was your husband after all, but it's beginning to get on my nerves. What kind of person throws the whole burden onto a weak woman? That's how it was when he was alive and that's how he behaves after death. Coming in dreams with demands. He was never a good person, that Volf. You're allowed to tell the truth even about the dead."

Soreh-Gitl's elongated, shriveled face stretches down to its hard, pointy chin. She clasps her Turkish shawl more tightly about her as if it has suddenly gotten colder.

"Don't speak like that, Ratse. What could he do? Volf was always a refined person. Always had to have the spoon at the right time to eat. Suffered no aggravation. Well, you know what he had to endure because of his son. Since they took Moshke and he saw him carried away. His blood froze. His years were cut short on account of that young man. Now he can't even rest in the grave. He's still a father after all."

Ratse lights a candle and places it under the slanting eave of the kitchen.

"A good week!"

"A good week to you as well. May my children give me something to be proud of!" Soreh-Gitl groans.

"As long as it's not bad, that would make it good. Then it would *have* to be good," Hersh Lustik interjects from the doorway. He shakes of his Sabbath kapote, walks over to the glass-paned cupboard, and busies himself there for a bit. He takes the spice box and sings in a low voice:

> *Va-yiten lekho*—
> Money there is none;
> *Mishmanei ho-orets*—
> The money's at the lord's;
> *Ve-royv dogon*—
> You'll still get a good slugging.[42]

Give us the news, Soreh-Gitl."

"What news can I give? I still can't cope with the old man."

"You're not going to tell *me* any tales, Soreh-Gitl. If you've made it to another good week, it wasn't for nothing," Hersh Lustik says, scrunching his left eye mischievously.

Soreh-Gitl undoes her Turkish shawl and gets up in a hurry.

"To cut a long story short, Hersh, I came to talk some sense into Tsvetl. Volf's been getting no rest in the grave. You should know, Hersh—we're no strangers after all—I don't much like Tsvetl. They've got to cover that girl's head. I fear for a ring. Give me some advice, Hersh, about what I should do."

Lustik drums his fingers on the bare table.

"Giving women advice? Not inclined toward that. But if some advice were given—why shouldn't Bertshik put a ring on her finger? Let him give her a ring and recite the verse."

The hair stands up under Soreh-Gitl's wig, her face aflame. She lunges at Hersh, ready to claw his eyes out.

"What did you say, Hersh?! Bertshik should be my son-in-law? Bertshik Shmatte? Over my dead body!"

She draws the shawl over her head and sobs.

"Have I fallen so low in people's estimation? Why is this happening to me? To Volf in the grave? When a husband dies, his wife has nothing more to live for."

Hersh calmly blows smoke rings up under the low ceiling.

"Well, try understanding women. Why don't you like Bertshik? He's got a nice room, he does a good business running to the village, can keep a wife fed. He's become practically an aristocrat! Yisrultshe Blimeles is looking for someone pedigreed for his daughter. Could just as well give him the Maharal for a son-in-law.[43] Now he's bursting with bitterness. Soreh-Gitl, if it's pedigree you're really looking for, Tsvetl will end up the same as Khashe with the blind eye with her Grunem. She pops out a house-full of children while he—begging your pardon—makes his apologies and sets off on the road."

Ratse is standing by the little stove, crumbling bits of chicory between her fingers and sprinkling them into the pan. She turns around towards her husband.

"Hersh, don't force her. If Soreh-Gitl doesn't want Bertshik, you shouldn't make her. In matters of matchmaking you mustn't interfere. I would just like to know one thing, Soreh-Gitl, what have you got to criticize Bertshik about?"

"Ratse, you too? You've got to be stronger than iron to endure this. He's involved with 'sinful' women. Wherever there's a tavern, there you'll find Bertshik. Where there's stolen goods, there's Bertshik. And what a face that one's got! Of course it's the loser who goes right for me. What a girl! Didn't go getting besotted with anyone else, just that Bertshik. She knows what she's like with him. He tells her: 'Tsvetl, three and sixteen a ticket; go to Warsaw and get a job as a maid.' No, dear brother-in-law, from that grain no bread can be made. I am not a fan. Nor is Volf in his grave. It'll all go up in smoke for us."

Hersh Lustik rubs his freezing fingers.

"But Soreh-Gitl, you don't throw the baby out with the bathwater. You're not going to tell *me* any tales. You've likely already got someone for Tsvetl at the ready?"

Soreh-Gitl makes an angry face.

"Who do I have at the ready? I have no one at the ready. I've got no secrets from you. But if Tsvetl follows my advice she'll accept Harshl. You know who I mean. That young man from Grodzisk."

"So that's it? That's the story? You really do have a match for Tsvetl. What Harshl? Harshl the bootmaker?"

"Harshl the bootmaker. He's a quiet young man and an orphan. So he's *not* especially handsome. Where is it written that a man must be handsome?"

Girlish laughter drifts in from the courtyard. Children throwing snowballs. People run from upper storeys down the wooden stairs. From every which way doors open. Khashe with the blind eye comes running from Yisrultshe Blimeles' yard. She yells her throat out over the dry frost, "Shloymele, Shloymele, go home! Why are you bothering the girls? You're still just a boy scrambling around in the dirt. Just you wait, I'll tell your father on you. Grunem, Grunem! The boy's going around pestering people!"

In the little entryway, someone is stamping their feet, shaking off the snow. The door opens suddenly. Tsvetl tumbles in, half-dead, and Pesele after her. They wipe the snow from their faces. Tsvetl, covered in snow, smoothes her damp, blonde hair. She's angry.

"Don't you get it? What a brat! Pelting me all over with snow."

Pesele, thirteen years old with tresses combed in tight knots around her ears, and blue, dreamy eyes, says in a huff, "And he *pinched* me, the little pest."

Hersh looks at Pesele cheerfully, his face beaming, his eyes alight with a paternal sparkle.

"Come here, my little girl. Come sit on your uncle's knee. I'll give that Shloymele a thrashing to remember. Pesele, give your uncle a kiss."

Soreh-Gitl squirms in her Turkish shawl. Her elongated face stretches even longer.

"Kissing? A girl of thirteen doesn't kiss men."

"Am I a man then, Pesele? An uncle is certainly not a man. One's allowed to kiss an uncle."

Hersh bursts out laughing and catches Pesele by the arm. Pesele wrestles with her uncle. Ratse removes the pan of boiled milk from the chafing rings and shakes her head at her husband.

"Dimwit, leave the girl alone! As it is, we've got none of our own."

Soreh-Gitl rebukes Tsvetl, "Can't leave them alone for a minute. How is this obeying me?"

Tsvetl smoothes her hair in the mirror.

"The yarn broker came by. He's going to cut the prices again. In Garwolin two hundred girls are striking. Tomorrow I'm throwing my work aside."

"And who did you forget about while you were with that broker? We'll be left in poverty."

Tsvetl shrugs her shoulders.

"There's Harshl; for all I know he's just sitting there rolling cigarettes."

One of Hersh's eyes is laughing; the other is squinting.

"That so, Tsvetl? Breaking down the doors are they? Prospective grooms coming and going. You'll be good again after all, Soreh-Gitl."

"May it be no better for my enemies."

Tsvetl grimaces.

"Just the thought of it, Harshl a groom! If he comes, then there he'll be; I'm obviously not going to throw him out. But Uncle," she says with a sour look on her face, "he's a ginger."

Once again Soreh-Gitl loses her temper.

"So what if he's a ginger? With Bertshik all you'll get are rings under your eyes. At least the other one's a provider, without a father or a mother."

Tsvetl shrugs her shoulders.

"Stop nagging me with his selling points. Auntie Ratse, what are you cooking up there? I love Ratse's food."

Soreh-Gitl heads for the door. Pesele is sitting on the bench bed, cracking up with laughter at what her uncle has been whispering to her. Tsvetl helps her aunt flip the latkes in the frying pan, as she taps her feet and hums a song:

> My mother went into the street for coal and
> Brought me back a lad from Poland.
> Oho what a lad, so handsome and so fine,
> What lovely eyes he's got, darling of mine.

22

WHERE SOMEONE'S
GOT THE "NERVES"

A fresh frost invigorates the rising day. Wholesome wintry sunlight shines into Yisrultshe Blimeles' yard. Crowns of precious gems sparkle down from the little windows. But Grunem neither sees nor feels any of it. Those senses are all dulled. One couldn't blame Khashe, his wife with the blind eye. She *actually* couldn't see. Her other eye has also started clouding over. Any little grief and it would start watering, the tears flowing like a spring. Everyone knows that Khashe with the blind eye is already a lost cause. But Grunem is still a young man, never in a hurry. *Grunem is Grunem, with the boyish punim.*[44] Sometimes his face seems to laugh and sometimes it looks like it's about to cry. That misfortunate Grunem, a father of six children, has no trace of a beard.

Despite how badly things have gone for her, Khashe still has her wits about her. She tucks the children in with pillows. Leaves them in bed till midday. Not only is it warm, but there their hunger also fades. But the fact that Grunem, a grown man, should lie stretched out in bed till ten o'clock is something Khashe cannot understand, so she stations herself next to him by the bed, unyielding, and pours out her troubles:

"Grunem, why are you just lying there? Grunem, why are you yawning? People are bustling about. This one in and that one out. Wheeling and dealing. And you, Grunem? Dearest bread-winner of mine! A house with seven souls. I'm not even counting myself. But for the little ones, Grunem, the little ones . . ."

Grunem is playing with their youngest child, Hadassah. He takes off the blanket, petting her little crooked legs and lifting her into the air. The little girl winces from the cold and buries herself in her father's chest. Grunem lays her back down and rolls a cigarette from homemade tobacco leaves. The smoke irritates Khashe's good eye. It starts watering as if someone has suddenly opened the sluice of a dammed river. Zlatke, with tangled, feather-strewn locks, having slept poorly, sits on the edge of the bed and looks out the frozen window at the little yard. A smile plays about her dark, girlish face.

"Mama, mama. Just look what kind of sun there is today."

Khashe blinks both sickly eyes.

"Sun and rain. The girls in this house are growing. Grunem, maybe enough lazing about?"

Grunem gets down off the bed. He stands there in his night-clothes, distracted, his skin wrinkled and quivering like a fish.

"Khashe, I don't know why you woke me up. My business deals aren't going to run away."

"But the years are running away, Grunem. The children are growing up. *Do* something, Grunem. See about earning some-thing. Khone Baker wouldn't give me any rolls. After all, you have to look at it from his position. How long can he give things on credit? I've worked myself pretty well for you, Grunem. You reap what you sow."

Grunem picks at his naked chin in confusion.

"But Khashe, what can one accomplish with empty pockets? If only my father-in-law would give me a couple of hundred zlotys . . ."

Khashe suddenly jumps from her seat, her eyes as red as fire.

"But he's given us money. Haven't you taken enough dowries? You've shortened my father's life. He's an old man. Just one father, poor thing. I don't have another. Money, money . . . A scam with money. Do something *without* money!"

Grunem gets dressed. His frayed black kapote is tight, and he can't reach his hand to his shoulder. He spins around like that for quite some time, like a cat after its tail.

"If I had just three hundred zlotys I'd open a little grocery store."

"A store, a store," Khashe shakes her head. "You've already had stores. And you still owe 33-years' taxes."

"I mean a market stall with blue dishes. I'd travel the fair circuit."

Khashe wrings her hands.

"With blue dishes he's going to do a business for me in the market. Oh, my big shot! And what if a brawl breaks out and you've got to flee the fair? After all, you've still got a hernia from when you were conscripted."

Grunem's smooth, hairless face turns bright red.

"You're not supposed to mention my affliction. Do you hear, Khashe? Blind bat!"

Khashe beats her fist against her flour-spattered blouse, sending up a cloud of flour that spreads through the room and catches in the throat.

"So I'm blind am I? And who made me blind if not you?"

She cries in choked sobs.

"What a family. All sickly people. Gitl in America's got the *nerves* in her heart, Grine in Sorczew's got the *nerves* in her feet, and Khashe's got the *nerves* in her eyes. No one chooses it. It's fate . . ."

Grunem smiles contentedly.

"So I'm telling you the same thing, that you lot are an unwell family. Since I met you it's all gone pear-shaped. As a lad I was ambitious, a go-getter, always had silver coins in my pocket."

The children start bickering over a dried flower seed. Little Hadassah scoots across the floor mumbling, *"Petshe-metshe, metshe-petshe."* They are all tangled together in a ball. You could see nothing but dirty little shirts. Grunem removes his belt to give Shloymele a licking; with one hand he holds up his pants, and with the other he strikes his son. Khashe runs to her husband, blindly beating her fists on his shoulders.

"Murderer, anti-Semite! What do you want from the boy? How many boys do I have? Only one son![45] Grunem, may your hands wither! Grrrrrunem, I'll scream bloody murder and people will come running!"

Shloymele, his face scratched, tears himself away from his father's clutches, looking around with wild goggling eyes as if searching for something.

"Father shmather," he says through gritted teeth. Running over to the sideboard he throws the oil lamp onto the floor, sticking his long red tongue out at his father, and in two bounds is outside in the frost.

Khashe sits down next to the stove and starts peeling potatoes. Her fingers are trembling. She feels the skin of the potato, looking for the eyes and cutting them out with the peeler. She says to herself, "Had a dolman for my wedding, a plush jacket . . . gold rings . . . musicians played . . ."

Grunem goes to the kitchen, laying his hand on the lid of the cold teapot. His boyish face grimaces.

"At least there could be a little boiled water. A swig of tea."

Khashe harangues the pot of potatoes.

"Tea, tea, tea. I give him tea. Not used to anything else. It's fine for me without tea, too."

"That's just your luck, Khashe. What've you got against me?"

"*My* luck? It's *your* luck. After all, I'm living off your merits, oh helpmate of mine!"

Her eyes start watering again. Patches of naked skin are visible through her blouse. Grunem remembers how different Khashe looked at their wedding. Her body was white and she could see out of both eyes. He wants to say something nice to her, but his mouth has gone dry. He couldn't hear his own voice. So he turns his collar up to his ears, kisses the mezuzah, and leaves.

23

GRUNEM DEALS IN HONEY

He enters the courtyard where the fruit sellers live in order to get some advice from Hersh Lustik. It's a cozy place, Hersh Lustik's. The turf crackles cheerfully under the little stove, and the canary twitters in its cage above the window. Hersh is sitting at the sewing machine in his undershirt, stitching pants. Ratse is swiftly sewing on the buttons. The marketplaces have grown quieter. The St. Marcin Fair is coming up and they're short on ready material. Hersh, his sleeves rolled up, is churning out one pair of pants after another, all the while singing a little tune:

> *I am a little Hasid, a very cheerful soul,*
> *I am a little Hasid, guileless on the whole.*
> *I am a little Hasid, I dance and I hop,*
> *All in my little prayer shawl, hop-chop-chop.*

The door never rests. People keep coming in and going out. As the machine clacks away people give him a talking-to. It all soon starts going in one ear and out the other. Soreh-Gitl stands there in her Turkish shawl demanding justice. Her diminutive, sallow face has shrunk even more, and her hard, bony chin has grown even pointier. Volf had come to her again in a dream. So there she stands, her chin leaning over the machine.

"Hersh, I've really got no one left except you, a lone brother-in-law. Say something, quick, *do* something. She's certainly persistent, Tsvetl. She knows she's fallen in with Bertshik, while Harshl worships the ground she walks on. Hersh, I need something for a sewing machine, for a quarter of the rent, for a couple of beds. Y'gather the necessaries, break a plate, cover the girl's head, and the marriage contract's done. Hersh, nothing good will come of waiting. Believe me, my dear brother-in-law, we can't wait any longer."

Hersh raises his head from the machine.

"And Bertshik's good with such an arrangement?"

Soreh-Gitl's pointy chin gets even pointier.

"I shouldn't have sinned by complaining; but he's already skimmed off the cream. What more does he need? Could you have expected this, Hersh? Volf's daughter, eh?"

The machine stops as if on its own. Hersh remains seated, motionless. His hollow voice sounds as if coming from an empty barrel.

"Whoever skims the cream should drink the clabber. Let her get married to Bertshik! That's how it's done among us Jews."

Soreh-Gitl's face contorts into a grimace.

"But that's the problem, Hersh. Bertshik's stalling. We can't wait any longer. And whenever I try talking to him he just answers curtly, 'Three and sixteen a ticket. Let her go to Warsaw.' Now he's fallen off the map. We know nothing about what's become of him. Just tell us what we need to do. Maybe a lawsuit? Determined 'Such and such' . . . 'Insulted the Polish people' . . ."

Grunem slips inside with a dry little cough. A bit of frost blows in after him. Hersh turns around, his shoulder toward the sewing machine.

"Hello, Grunem. How are things now that you're living in the new place at your father-in-law's?"

Grunem stands by the glowing stove, warming his hands over the flame.

"Thank you for asking, Hersh. It's going very well. Aside from a livelihood I'm not lacking anything."

"Ah, livelihood, livelihood," Hersh says, taking his grizzled beard in his hand. "Jews are strange people. Just give them a livelihood. Without it they won't budge."

Grunem's naked face reflects the light of the fire.

"You must understand, Hersh, there's no work to be had. Simply nothing. I would already have gotten the couple of hundred zlotys from my father-in-law. My family doesn't want to let me stand in the middle. But what trade to take up? I'm thinking of opening a haberdashery. What do you think, Hersh? Would that offer a means of support, haberdashery?"

Hersh shrugs.

"I'm not going to persuade you. So what is haberdashery? Something you abhor and trash . . ."

Grunem scratches the left side of his face where on all Jews, including him, there's supposed to be a side lock.

"Or maybe a wine shop? Passover's approaching. If I can get a little wine from Hungary . . ."

Hersh Lustik looks at Soreh-Gitl, at her gloomy face, and all at once thinks of what Bertshik told him at the fair, that they had stuck him in prison in Płock. He answers Grunem, "What good's a wine shop to you, Grunem? What good's Hungary to you? Truth be told, it's all the same to you whether you're hungry or not."

A tubercular smile appears on Grunem's dark face.

"Hersh, I find the world very cramped. What does one *do*? Six hungry mouths. A crippled wife. At least it would be useful to her. Not so the both of us . . ."

"True, true." Hersh shakes his head. "You're good when it comes to circumcisions. But having children's not a trade, it's wisdom. When you finally open a shop, Grunem, it's all just trifles, unsteady and insecure. What you're looking for is a livelihood that will last."

"Such as? By all means, what do you suggest?"

Hersh rubs his forehead. Then a light goes on in his mind. His face beams.

"Your father-in-law has a yard with a garden?"

"True."

"Flowers grow in Yisrultshe Blimeles' garden?"

"They do."

"In my grandfather Nisn Kretshmer's garden in Boża Wola there were beehives. Whole caskfuls of mead were sent down the Vistula to Danzig. Grunem, set up a couple of beehives in your father-in-law's garden. Get ready for the summer. I'm a fruit seller, Grunem, so I know about such things. I'll show you how the first time. The German Witbrot will give you a couple of beehives. I'll convince him."

Grunem's flat face twists into a grimace.

"Ha, ha, ha, Hersh. How'd you get that idea? What good is honey to Jews? Rosh Hashanah is still a long way away. But my family needs bread now."

"I'm sticking to my advice, Grunem. If you're looking for something serious, something about which no one will say 'Don't do it,' then take up honey. And don't worry, Grunem, Jews like sweets. We'll get it announced in the synagogue that people should eat honey. 'If things are bitter, at least you can have a little something sweet.' Go home and talk it over with your wife. Khashe will let you. Why shouldn't she?"

Grunem with his empty stomach is enticed by the smell of honey. He could taste the sweetness in his mouth and starts considering various stratagems to persuade his father-in-law. He would tell his family: "Until now you've given money for nothing; now you'll be giving money for honey." He throws himself on Hersh, grabbing his hand.

"Well done, Hersh, thank you!"

"Don't mention it," Hersh says, extracting himself from Grunem's arms. "You can thank me later. You can treat me with some honey. Go home now, and do what I told you."

24

TSVETL

Somewhere between a yes and a no Tsvetl has become Harshl the bootmaker's wife. No one knows how that happened. Tsvetl herself doesn't know. Tall, with a slender waist, golden hair, dark, almond eyes, black brows, and an easy gait—whom does Tsvetl resemble? Well, Tsvetl's grandfather, Volf's father, traded in wood and had dealings with the Prince. He had beautiful daughters. All of them helped in his business, and the girls were called the Prince's grandchildren. So when Tsvetl walks through the Smolin marketplace with a bundle of sweaters, everyone watches her.

"The beautiful knitter-girl."

When Tsvetl discusses something it's down to the minute. She doesn't make excuses. Her dainty mouth stretches into a sweet little laugh.

"I can't be held up when I know they're waiting for me."

She is envious of nothing and keeps nothing hidden. A kiss, a pet. Let the young people enjoy themselves. And what's more, there's the matter of Bertshik Shmatte. How has Bertshik with the dark, showy mustache and piercing little eyes come to attain Tsvetl? Tsvetl herself doesn't know the answer to that. But she does know that he had captivated her from the very first moment. When her father was ill, instead of taking care of him she ran off to see Bertshik, reading him interesting little pieces from the newspapers, from novels like *The Beggar Countess* or *The Sinful Priest*. Tsvetl knows Bertshik indulges himself too often with others. She is nevertheless devoted to him. That's what she wants. After all, for her part she is genteel and refined. Bertshik is due a bonus. Every Sabbath evening, after a stroll beyond the mill, she would come home with blue marks under her eyes. Tsvetl knows Bertshik is never going to marry her.

"I wanna be a free man. And you yourself, Tsvetl, what good's it do you to drive yourself crazy over all that wedding business and the musicians when you've already got everything you need?" Bertshik says, with both hands in the pockets of his suede pants and squinting his left eye mischievously.

Tsvetl doesn't respond because she doesn't want to contradict Bertshik. But deep within her there still glows a spark of hope that Bertshik would grow up and long for his own home.

Her mother Soreh-Gitl scolds her.

"Tsvetl, from that grain no bread can be made. That young man's driving you mad for no good reason. Bertshik still has locks to break."

And her uncle Hersh chimes in, "So let it be Bertshik. But how much longer do you have to wait? Let it last a year and come to an end. After all, nothing will come of just going along."

Tsvetl laughs archly, right in her uncle's face.

"So something's got to happen soon?"

"Some fine *soon*; this *soon*'s already been *soon* for two years and there's no end in sight."

The tight widow's-bonnet on Soreh-Gitl's head trembles.

After some time, Harshl the bootmaker arrives, which frightens Tsvetl at first. A ginger! With one leg shorter than the other and slow of speech. Lacking any assertiveness, shy. No understanding of how to treat a girl.

"Here's my 'pal,' treat him well!" Bertshik says, in a half-commanding, half-comradely way as he ushers him into the house.

Soreh-Gitl pounces as if on a warm roast.

"A quiet young man, a good earner, not a profligate, and an orphan to boot."

Tsvetl's blonde head trembles.

"Am I responsible for his being an orphan? Anyway, I can't be his mother."

"Not a mother, Tsvetl, just a wife. A wife as God commanded. Because you and Bertshik . . . May I not be punished for speaking . . . Better not get me started talking, daughter."

Then there came the engagement feast followed by the wedding. But the morning after the wedding Harshl starts grumbling. Tsvetl lowers her eyes for shame.

"But you knew I was with Bertshik."

Harshl gets angry. His sallow face turns as red as copper. He gnashes his teeth and tosses his disheveled hair.

"They're going to know, they're going to know."

Now Tsvetl gets mad.

"So they're going to know. I didn't beg you."

Harshl grabs a pair of bootlegs, shakes them out on the floor, and stamps on them. Seeing that, Tsvetl takes the basket containing her trousseau and goes home to her widowed mother and bursts into tears.

"It's how you wanted it, mother, just what you wanted. To bury me alive."

Weeks pass. Tsvetl's bed in the couple's home remains made. Her photograph, the one where she is dressed in her veil, looks down from over the sideboard with importunate eyes. It makes Harshl ill. The neighbors notice how the housework is being neglected and Harshl has shrunk to a shadow of himself. They send for Lustik so he might reconcile things. So Hersh comes over, sizes Harshl up with a couple of keen glances, and chides him companionably.

"You're acting childishly, Harshl. What's done is done. You mustn't spoil today because of what happened yesterday. If you didn't love Tsvetl, that'd be something different. Jews find a way. But you, Harshl, you *do* love her. The whole hullabaloo is *because* you love her. It'll pass, Harshl, it'll pass."

Harshl turns toward the shelf and cries his manly eyes out. Taking this as a sign of progress, Hersh takes Harshl by the hand, leads him in to Soreh-Gitl, and instructs her to get a bottle of brandy and egg cookies.

25

KHASHE WITH THE BLIND EYE WANTS OPEN DOORS

When it's quiet at Khashe's, the neighbors know that Grunem has gone. Then windows get opened and people air out their homes. Khashe's body is well-rested. She sleeps like a lord, in the same bed as Hadassah. The other three girls she packs into Grunem's bed, and she makes a pallet for Shloymele on the floor. Khashe would never have believed it could be so good without a man. It would have been better still but for Shloymele. He dismisses everyone, talks back to grown-ups, and makes trouble with the whole town. The upshot is it all gets piled onto Khashe's head. She loses the weekly allowance from her sister Sheva, Shmuel Loyvithser's wife. Khone Baker doesn't want to give her the seven weekly rolls on her father's account. But Khashe keeps quiet. Because she understands that's how people are. They're just looking for how to squeeze her. Her neighbors lecture her:

"When you've got such a loser of a husband, you mustn't be so outspoken. You've got to show people some respect. You've got to bend, Khashe. Bend!"

Khashe's good eye starts watering again.

"I've bent enough. I've taken people's guff. Better the bitter from God than the sweet from people. My little sister . . . When she gets the opportunity to take a jab at me she does. Stopped the weekly allowance. What did I do to deserve this? After all, she's always been cold towards me. Do you see, my son, the trouble you've caused?"

So once Grunem has gone off toward Cyncymin to see Hersh Lustik in his orchard and learn from the German Witbrot the ins and outs of making honey, Shloymele goes to see Khone Baker, and says churlishly, in his shrill little voice, "Khone, my grandpa pays you good money. We don't want your stale bread. You should be giving us fresh bread. All the rest of Smolin eats fresh bread."

Khone Baker has just finished pulling together a large table-ful of dried rolls for the rabbi on the Jewish community's account. Hearing this speech of Shloymele's, Khone's pale, sleepy face turns as red as a stove. He puts his hand to his ear and, like a tuning fork, tests to see if his hearing's alright.

"Eh? Insolent brat, what did you say? It's beneath you to eat stale bread? It's fine for the rabbi, but for you beggars it's not good enough?! You hearing this, Elka? Grunem's son wants fresh bread. Didn't I know it'd be like this? Well, Khashe made her bed, now she has to sleep in it."

Then Elka, Khone's wife, goes up to Yisrultshe Blimeles' place to see old Zisl and stir up trouble.

That's the first dust-up.

The next morning, Thursday, Shloymele goes to see Aunt Sheva for the weekly allowance. Sheva is helping a difficult customer in the store so she has Shloymele wait. He waits an hour, then two. Khashe sends one child after another to see what's taking so long. Shloymele can hardly wait any longer. He grits his little teeth. Finally Sheva cuts two yards of fabric for her customer, writes the debt in her account book, takes two zlotys from the drawer, and gives them to him with a sigh.

"Here, give this to your mother and tell her that from now on I won't be able to give her more than two zlotys a week."

Shloymele jumps right up into her face.

"Auntie, do you also live on two zlotys a week?"

Sheva's hands starts trembling as her face turns blue.

"Tell your mother, when she starts working as hard as I do with my customers, then she'll get more too."

Just then Yisrultshe Blimeles returns home from the synagogue. While still in the doorway, kissing the mezuzah, his eyes glaze over and he lets out a moan.

"*Zisl*, I'm a goner!"

Leaning on her cane, old Zisl hobbles over to her husband.

"What's wrong, Yisrultshe? Maybe you need a powder? Is it the asthma again?"

Yisrultshe lowers himself heavily into a chair.

"Powders . . . powders . . . Enough powders. I've got such joy in my golden years: Shloymele broke another window in the synagogue. My heart is failing me, Zisl."

"Of course it is when you wait till midday to eat. It's already twelve o'clock. That grandson. He's going to drive us into the grave yet. He ruined my goose-schmalz."

Yisrultshe slaps his hands together.

"Oh, dear! Sweet Father in heaven. At a time like this. What, all the holiday goose-schmalz, gone?"

"Not gone, just gone bad. She's your daughter after all, Yisrultshe. Not another one like that in the world. Some *wychowanie* you gave your kids, some upbringing! To take a dead cat and throw it into a house. We're well recompensed, Yisrultshe. I have six snakes hanging over my head and Khashe is the seventh."

Yisrultshe washes his hands before eating. He hasn't even managed to dip his hard challah in the salt when Khashe arrives unexpectedly and stands in the doorway. He turns toward his daughter and chokes on the challah.

"Eh, Khashe, what're you here for?"

Khashe steels herself with effort.

"No reason, papa. Am I not allowed to come?"

"Why not? Sit down."

Khashe remains standing by the door, leaning with her elbow on the handle.

"Khone Baker won't give me any bread, papa."

Yisrultshe takes a sip of coffee. He adjusts the saltcellar. He is preparing himself to lecture his daughter.

"Is that the point, my daughter? I'm asking you. That husband of yours hightailed it away. And the burden falls onto me and these old bones of mine. Am I capable of giving you seven loaves a week, eh?"

Zisl wrinkles her nose.

"Fresh rolls! Can't exist on anything else. Eating butter. Just as long as it's buttered . . . spread with butter . . ."

Khashe takes a step forward.

"Papa, the world has grown dark for me. I've lost the bright light. Now my other eye is failing. Grunem said it's my miserable luck. Hadassah just sits there; four years old and she can't stand on her feet. Gabriel said she's got to get milk every day. She's got rickets. Papa, knock out a window, make room just for a little shop for me. An open door's all I need. Just an open door, out onto the street . . ."

Yisrultshe's face darkens. He starts kneading his beard.

"Knock out a window for them! Give them some open doors! Open doors! You've already had open doors. And what did you accomplish, eh? How many more dowries will be enough? Not enough to bleed your father dry? I married you off, yes or no? Got you a husband. Set you up in a house on the courtyard. You've got six children, may they be strong and healthy. Now you're expecting the seventh. What more could I have done for you?"

Khashe sobs aloud.

"Papa, the light's been taken from my eyes. My whole life you've treated me like a stranger. I was raised by relatives. I washed diapers for my aunts, anywhere you had sisters. I was a servant girl, a scullion, a chambermaid. There was no one to teach me anything. Neither to read or to write. Always either holding a broom in my hand or standing at the washtub scrubbing the laundry. Then you married me off. From the very first minute everything went wrong. The kasha mill went kaput. I'm going to have to pawn the last of the pillows. Now he's gotten obsessed with honey."

Yisrultshe groans.

"Oh, the grief of raising children! The pride and joy of my old age. The Almighty apparently wants to keep me going on a bit into my declining years. Daughter, what do you want of me in my final years? Grunem's got to learn that if you can't go over you have to go under. Nothing's going to come of that honey. Lustik's gotten him all worked up for nothing. Jews don't put much stock in honey. Let him do some teaching. He's profligate, that husband of yours. Smoking cigarettes, singing 'Bney Heykholo'— considering himself one of the burghers." [46]

Khashe wipes her eyes with her sleeve. Her eyes are an active spring; they never run dry.

"Papa, why did you not pick a craftsman for my husband? Then I'd be saved . . ."

Yisrultshe wrings his hands.

"You see, there you're right, my daughter. That's my fault. In this I am responsible. One mustn't pity one's children. As it is written, You shall not look with pity . . . [47] And I, fool that I am, wanted to get you a respectable husband, a scholar. But one has to harden one's heart. Khone Baker will start giving you seven rolls a week again. And what else? Was that the point? You've got growing children . . ."

"A tiny little store, papa, just a tiny little store," Khashe sobs. "An open door out onto the marketplace. It went badly, God help me, from the very first minute. Grunem got himself a harness and the horse up and died. He set up a kasha mill and people started importing kasha from abroad. He started pickling eggs and egg prices hit rock-bottom. Now I don't even know if the bees will make any honey."

"Don't you see at last?" Yisrultshe says triumphantly. "That's just your luck. Every day you'll get a loaf from Khone."

"Yes, dearest papa, that's my luck. No one else's, just mine. My miserable luck."

Khashe heads for the door, consoled . . .

26

HERSH LUSTIK BECOMES A BAL-BRIS[48]

The days between Passover and Shavuot have returned to Smolin. Merchants with their wives and daughters stand in the doorways of their shops, their eyes on the lookout for gentile customers. Being idle, they look over towards the wooden hut on the other side of the marketplace. There is more commotion there than usual. And something new to boot: a sign over the gateway with bootlegs painted on it that Harshl the bootmaker had hung out. The courtyard is occupied by fruit sellers and produce traders who have stopped going from village to village. They are living off last year's potatoes and the sorrel leaves that grow wild along the fences in Smolin. They rack their brains trying to figure out how such a thing could have happened. Nothing had come of the meeting. Grunem, who interprets everything for the worse, thinks the "treasury" is preparing for an inspection or even an execution. Khashe, who loves attending weddings and funerals, blinks her blind eye.

"Folks, did you hear? May it not happen, but someone has just passed from this world."

When Shmuel Loyvitsher's wife Sheva, the dry goods seller, hears that, her sweet little mouth twists.

"I'd say it's a wedding; there are only young couples living in that courtyard. But a funeral? It's too quiet for that." She slides the red kerchief down piously over her hair. "Or an inspection? But who's got anything to take? What'll they find among the produce sellers? Eighteen farthings and a wooden hump. Hersh Lustik always carries around that tobacco tin, and with Ratse's flannel pants that's all they've got. Not an execution either. Stands to reason. Just an old sewing machine, kaput. Only good for scrap. Nothing else nowadays."

Hersh Lustik, tall and slim, runs across the marketplace, coattails spread like the sails of a windmill. Into one house and out of another. He doesn't run so much as caper impishly, like a boy. No, no one has died in Hersh Lustik's courtyard. It's hard to stop him because he's in such a hurry, which is not his wont. But Lazar Kurnik, who has nothing but time on his hands, has to try and figure it all out. So he grabs Hersh by the coattail.

"Hersh, why the rush? What's the special occasion?"

Hersh frees himself from Lazar's grasp.

"I've got no time, my dear man. Today I'm a *bal-bris*."

People hold their sides as uproarious laughter breaks out across the marketplace.

"Hersh Lustik a *bal-bris*?"

"At his age?"

"Barren Ratse's given birth to a son?"

Hersh Lustik emerges from School Street. Accompanying him is mute Khayim's wife, Yitte, Bertshik's mother, wobbling from hip to hip like a duck. Yitte has a small dairy in mute Khayim's old courtyard. She makes little cheeses from heated sour milk, and sells cottage cheese and cream for three and six groschens apiece. She is quite elderly, with gummy eyes, and she wears a bonnet covered with a great many ribbons. Because of her stammering husband, mute Khayim, she has long forgotten how to speak. But Yitte performs many good deeds. She makes incantations to ward off the Evil Eye, rubs liniments on children's bellies when there's an epidemic making the rounds, gathers bean leaves for abscesses, and attends to women whose labor pains have begun. Now Hersh Lustik is leading this ninety-year-old woman into the courtyard of the fruit sellers. Someone is giving birth. That's clear to everyone. But who? Obviously not Ratse. Then Sheva suddenly claps her hands together.

"Y'hear what I'm telling you, people? It's Tsvetl. Tsvetl the boot-stitcher's wife. But something just doesn't add up. The wedding was around Hanukkah and now it's near Lag b'Omer.[49] So wait just a moment . . ."

She slides her red kerchief down even more piously and starts counting the months on her fingers: *Kislev, Tevet, Shvat, Adar, Nisan, Iyar.*

"So, *that*'s the story! It's good that Soreh-Gitl got that girl's head covered just in time."

Lazar Kurnik couldn't stand hearing a Jewish girl being besmirched.

"What's the d-d-d-iff'r'nce when she got married, Hanukkah or Purim? As long as Hersh Lustik's family's blessed with a boy, eh? Look here, Doctor Gabriel's coming. That's no easy childbirth then."

Hersh scurries around the whole day. Here someone is lending him a hot-water bottle, there an ice bucket, now someone is bringing him a cup of chicken broth for the woman in labor. And here is Grunem running over to him with a packet of Psalms for the mother's protection.[50] Sheva loves her good deeds so she cooks a pot of boiled peas for the feast on the Sabbath before the circumcision.

"If not the birth then at least the circumcision will be as God commanded!" she whispers to the other women.

Soreh-Gitl, Tsvetl's mother, is ill with rheumatism, so Ratse fusses around the laboring mother: putting a cleaver under her pillow, covering the bed with sheets, nailing up the evil-averting Psalms, sending for Grunem to inspect the mezuzah to see if it's ritually fit. After all, it isn't the first time Ratse has been on the case with a woman in labor. She had married off all of Hersh's nieces and nephews, was there when they gave birth, and helped when their children were weaned. It was only her womb that God closed up. No children's little mouths had ever bitten her nipples so they are as fresh and perky as a young girl's. Her breasts, however, are thin and shriveled, not full like those of nursing mothers. Day by day they grow more wrinkled as if ashamed of their solitude. She stands lost in thought for minutes on end, sometimes even forgetting she's supposed to be helping the mother. She could do nothing right today. Ratse suddenly feels completely superfluous in God's world.

Hersh is rushing around in a frenzy, completely out of character. He lays a warm hand on Ratse's back and looks over her shoulder at the baby with its little pink head and trembling, shut eyes as it lies next to its mother, moving its tiny lips like a fish on dry ground gulping for air. Hersh's eyes beam with joy.

"Ratse, Ratse. Aren't you happy? Our family's gotten bigger. Another little boy born in my old age. A little boy, Ratse. A little son. A . . . a . . ."

Ratse couldn't get as excited as Hersh. But there are tears in her eyes. Tears of joy. Her husband's happiness is *her* happiness. But Ratse's tears don't please Hersh. His anger is simmering so he vents it on Harshl the stitcher who is standing by sullenly.

"Harshl!" he roars at him. "Harshl, why are you so gloomy today? Congratulations to you, Harshl. After all, you've become something of a father!"

Harshl lowers his disheveled red hair over a disassembled boot and, with an air of importance, closely examines the stitching he has just undone. His sleepy, hairy face is sunken and grim. His eyes stare sinisterly as he thinks malicious thoughts. This irritates Hersh, so he gets closer and pulls the visor of Harshl's hat down over his eyes. With a mocking look on his face he says, "Well papa, *bal-bris*, you've got a first-born son. Congratulations!"

Harshl the bootmaker lifts his head. His eyes are such as Hersh Lustik has never seen. He suddenly shakes his wild, unkempt hair, emitting a noise between his teeth that sounds like two empty pots grating against one another.

"Congratulations to you, Hersh, and extend my congratulations . . . to my dear 'pal' Bertshik."

These words deeply unsettle Hersh. His face stretches out, strangely elongating like his walking stick.

"Eh?" he asks in a distant, hollow voice. "What did you say, Harshl?"

He doesn't wait for an answer. Leaving Harshl to his unstitched bootlegs he quickly leaves the new mother's home as if fleeing a plague.

27

HERSH LUSTIK
DISTRIBUTES ALIYES[51]

V*e-eyleh*—"and these are"; *nesi'ey ho-eydoh*—"the influential
burghers of Smolin." *Yisrultshe Blimeles*. He achieves great
things for the sake of "the world to come, and lives from Sabbath
to Sabbath on a couple of stale loaves of challah and some plum
broth. *Shmuel Loyvitsher*. Yisrultshe's son-in-law, he owns a large
dry goods store, is the head of the Jewish community, and likes
sweets. The two of them know everyone. That still leaves: *Ber
Faytalovitsh*. He married off all his daughters, except the youngest, Ruzhke, who plays piano. Ber Faytalovitsh loans money to
the nobility. But since the moratorium on estate debts, among
all his properties he has opted for his seat in the synagogue. *Yosl
Katazhan*. He owns a brick building in the marketplace, a grain
warehouse. Embraces the Ten Commandments, except the
seventh. Once . . . From time to time . . . People don't talk
about it. Now a Hasid (with the finest silk kapote). Unexpectedly
at the last minute Yosl has become a member of the community

council and a regular at the administrative offices. *Itshe Shpilfoygl*. Timber merchant. Neither a Hasid nor a Zionist. In the middle. A Mizrahist.[52] So, until some upheaval turns things upside down, these are Smolin's leading citizens.

This is the order of the *aliyes*: *Kohen*—always Itshe Tshap, the letter writer, the left side of whose face is somewhat paralyzed. And he's a little hard of hearing. But he does remember very well the Turkish war: "Osman Pasha let himself be bribed."[53] He is the only *Kohen* in the synagogue. No disputes there. *Two* is the rabbi because he is a Levite. For *three* everyone concedes that it is Yisrultshe Blimeles' right. Whether because of his piety, or his eminence, or the fact that the synagogue cost him "a golden hen" (the money he set aside from denying himself food). *Five* was bought by Shmuel Loyvitsher, the head of the community. He only comes into the synagogue after the *Nishmas* prayer[54] because he has a nervous stomach so he has to have a snack before the morning service. (Khashe, Grunem's wife, has "nerves" in her eyes.) *Six*, meantime, belongs to Ber Faytalovitsh, because there's hope that the moratorium on estate debts might be repealed. As for *maftir*, there is an unspoken feud between Yosl, the newly minted council member, and Itshe Shpilfoygl, the old Mizrahist. The rest get the dregs: Torah-lifter, Torah-roller, *four*—these all fall to the folk, the common man. *Va-yiloynu hoom*[55]—"there was a grumbling afoot among the people." How is it just and how is it fair that all the best *aliyes* always go to the wealthy?!

Hersh Lustik has long considered correcting that injustice. Now he has been handed a timely opportunity. In the synagogue he is both Harshl the bootmaker's defender and the one who distributes the *aliyes*. The common people feel elevated. They are all arranged for their readings: Lazar Kurnik, Bertshik Shmatte, and Avreml "Treyf." Bertshik had spent half a year in the prison in Płock for supposedly having said "such and such" at the Wyszogród fair. Now he's standing in the synagogue, slim and dignified, and buoyant because of what he has endured for the sake of the Jews. He takes furtive glances over at Harshl the bootmaker who is sitting silent and hostile below the reading desk. He holds nothing against Harshl. It pleases him that Tsvetl, his former intended, has had a son, and that that son has a father, and that that father is Harshl the bootmaker. He doesn't hold grudges; he has already gone through the wringer.

So Itshe Tshap, the paralyzed letter writer, stays where he is: *Kohen*. For *Levi*, Hersh has Lazar Kurnik called. Night after night Lazar suffers on account of foreign wagons because he has no cart of his own. So once in a while he should get the pleasure of having a proper *aliye*. *Three*, as is customary, is given to Yisrultshe Blimeles. He's a pious Jew and a feeble man. It is forbidden to humiliate him. *Four* is received by Avreml "Treyf" who is back to slaughtering kosher. Bertshik Shmatte was an offering for the Jewish people, so Hersh lets him be called for *five*. Grunem has been hankering for a respectable *aliye* so he gets *six*.

But there is a dust-up over the *maftir*. All caused by Yosl Katazhan. It was a straightforward matter to grant *maftir* to Harshl the bootmaker. After all, he's a father and a *bal-bris*. Who could have imagined that Yosl would jump forward so authoritatively and threaten going to the police? Harshl himself doesn't even like being *maftir*. He walks like a stubborn ox to the slaughter with Hersh as his drover. In the middle of the blessing he starts choking. He keeps getting mixed up, switching the "who hath chosen" with the "who hath given."[56] He blushes as red as fire and breaks into a cold sweat. In that state he raises his mute eyes to the congregation, begging for help. But instead of setting him right and correcting which comes first and which comes after, what Harshl hears is something quite different. By the eastern wall, Yosl is talking about the bastards whose fathers are forbidden from entering the synagogue. Yosl has been itching for some time to lodge a complaint about *maftir*. But as long as Itshe Shpilfoygl had been on the opposing side he kept quiet. Itshe Shpilfoygl, though a Mizrahist, knows his Talmud. Yosl, on the other hand, had been exiled from Smolin as a young man, convicted for some very unsavory things. Now, however, he is a council member, and yet here they are, taking this person who no one knew how he had become a father and giving him *maftir*?! The ex-convict couldn't stand that. He bangs his fists on the reading desk and stamps his feet, not at all like a Hasid. Shmuel Loyvitsher, the head of the community, goads him, "Bertshik Shmatte . . . Anyone can get an *aliye*! The bone-picker . . . with a married woman . . ."

Yosl feels emboldened to even greater imperiousness, running up to Hersh and trying to push him from the reading desk. Seeing this, Harshl leaves the Torah scroll lying open and leaps at Yosl, choking him with his bear-like paws.

"Take that! Here's your bastards for you . . ."

Hasidim from the unified prayer house who had come into the synagogue to study come rushing over to defend Yosl, even though in their hearts they wish him, this ignoramus of a Hasid, nothing but ill. They swarm the reading desk in a knot. Bertshik Shmatte jumps over the lecterns, striding over heads and shoulders, ripping *tallises*, ensnaring his black nails in beards and side locks, and scratching faces. All his gentility evaporates like smoke. Clearly he is taking revenge for all the time he had spent in prison. Bertshik stops suddenly as if stricken lame. He feels the hard blows on his shoulder. It surprises him: how has such strength come to those pampered, rich-man's hands? But the blows don't stop. Bertshik notices a fist below his temple only when his eyes run with blood. No, these were intimate, comradely blows. Bertshik is overcome with pity for Harshl. So he lets him do what his heart desires and makes no attempt defend himself. The harder the blows the more he welcomes them.

Someone yells, "Water! Water!"

This causes Yisrultshe Blimeles to faint. A heavy book had been thrown at his head and he is now on the verge of giving up the ghost. Itshe Shpilfoygl and Ber Faytalovitsh are standing off to the side. The rabbi covers his ears and shakes his head at the fact that God's house has been transformed into a tavern. Everyone immediately rushes to revive Yisrultshe Blimeles. Yosl, all bloodied and his *tallis* in shreds, is panting heavily because of his fatty heart. He runs to the door. The police have arrived. At the sight of the blue uniforms the crowd is left standing with lowered eyes. Now Yosl takes charge of the synagogue. He staggers forward in his ripped *tallis* pointing his finger at Bertshik, at Avreml "Treyf," at Harshl.

"Take them away, *Panie Komisarzu*.[57] Arrest them! They're socialists. They sleep with foreign women."

Unable to tolerate such effrontery, Lazar Kurnik dredges up some old sins:

"Ex-con! Skirt-chaser! Thieving Hasid! Cavorting about with servant girls. Fattened swine! The grease is just dripping off your cheeks."

Gentiles start running over from the marketplace and mocking the way the Jews of Smolin pray.

In a corner of the synagogue, unnoticed by anyone, stands Gabriel Priver, observing his fellow townsmen. It isn't the first time he has taken to walking here. He has come to reassure himself; he takes every opportunity to feel the strength of his race. (Gabriel, too, has become accustomed to thinking in terms of race.) Now as always he suffers the consequences of letting himself be guided by his emotions. What he has seen in the Smolin synagogue today is more painful to him than the speeches he hears on the radio or the verdicts of the courts.

"Here's your Jewish people for you!" he hears someone ridicule him. "A chaotic, disorganized mass."

He observes the emaciated faces, fed on nothing but potatoes. The feeling of pity is rekindled in him; pity for these people who have been incited against one another by some outsider. No, they are not to blame for their benightedness. They are simply unlucky.

Harshl the bootmaker limps home on his short, bear-like legs. He wipes his sallow, bloodied face. Hersh comforts him.

"Harshl, I wanted you to enjoy life once in a while. Am I to blame that you weren't destined for *maftir*? That that ex-con got the Torah 'arrested'?"

Harshl lifts his head. For the first time, Hersh sees him with his shoulders level.

"Thanks, Hersh, for you good heart. I know you've been gracious to me; you weren't stingy with the *maftir*. But I gave the *maftir* today. I got even with Bertshik."

"Beautifully even," Hersh Lustik smiles as Harshl grimaces. "Gave him a nice black eye."

Harshl's sallow face once again floods with blind rage. He growls through his teeth, "He got me back worse, Hersh, much worse."

28

A HANGING BY NIGHT

What is the Smolin bell?

A piece of rusted metal with a wooden hammer. It doesn't bother Gabriel that the bell intrudes on the night. The barking of dogs spreads from all sides. The monotonous *bing-bong* in the darkness arouses no fear in him. But the people of Smolin are easily roused. The fear of fire, passed down to them from their forebears, runs in their blood. Bertshik Shmatte comes running first, wearing his brass helmet. Then comes Avreml "Treyf" with the forepart of a slaughtered ox over his shoulder. Lazar Kurnik arrives in his tight blue guard's tunic, with his under-*tallis* peeking out underneath. Itshe Tshap the letter writer drags himself along on his lame foot. And Hersh Lustik climbs up onto the pump and pierces the darkness with his eagle eyes.

"Nothing's burning. Just some soot smoking at the rebbetzin's."

"Where's it burning? What's burning?"

"May all our enemies burn."

Wherever there's a *malheur*, Grunem is the first one there. His slender body with its angular, bare face casts long shadows on the cobblestones. He's waving with both hands.

"People, what're you staring at? Why are you just standing there? There's been an accident. Ber Faytalovitsh . . ."

A large crowd has gathered in front of Ber Faytalovitsh's brick building. Women and children in their nightclothes are hanging out of the windows. Fear grows tenfold in the darkness. All eyes strain upward. From the middle of the ceiling, above the black piano, hangs Ber Faytalovitsh from a thick belt, his head lolling to the side. His chamois boots dangle below. A gold tooth sparkles from behind an upcurled lip. Between the gaps in his coat could be seen one lone *tzitzis*-fringe.[58]

"A doctor! A doctor!" comes the cry from all around. "Wake up the doctor. Why is he dozing when the whole town is *na platsu*, mustered on parade?!"

The noose is cut and Ber Faytalovitsh taken down. Gabriel Priver waves his hand.

"Send for the burial society."

He feels the hostile look from a girl's tearless eyes, proud and innocent. The eyes are dripping bitterness.

"Welcome. Imagine such a guest. He deigns to cross our threshold."

In front of the door people are talking amongst themselves in the bluish dawn.

"It weighed on Ber's heart. To have such wealth remain in Esau's hands."

"People are losing confidence; people are losing faith," Yisrultshe Blimeles groans. "To take one's own life. Ber, Ber, how could you have done such a thing?"

Grunem never takes his eyes from Ber's gold chain wound across his vest.

"I should own, together with twenty other Jews, however much money Ber had left with just one nobleman from Brzozów."

"Jewish wealth! One moratorium and it's bye-bye prosperity."

"It's a clever ruse. It drove Ber to an early grave."

"Whose genius idea was it?"

"It doesn't matter who as long as you get the dough, with your life or your soul," Hersh says as he buttons up his kapote to head home.

"Now Ruzhke has to get married to the nobleman from Brzozów. He's already got her dowry," jokes Bertshik Shmatte, angry at the bell for having disturbed him with his bride, who has a brother in America.

Lazar Kurnik adjusts the belt across his tunic. He plucks nervously at his long, straw-colored beard.

"I'm a neutral party. But if indeed we're now talking about Ber's daughter, then I have to ask you: Why, dear people, oughtn't she marry the doctor? The town should strive to make that happen. In any event, the brick building that Ber left behind is staying put."

Gabriel walks from one room to another, examining the pictures and antiques that Ber Faytalovitsh had spent a lifetime acquiring at auctions. His gaze falls on the black piano. Next to it, on a bit of sparsely strewn straw, lies Ber Faytalovitsh, covered in a black cloth. The candles in the open windows drip as the piano keys quiver in the breeze. Ruzhke, as pale as a white statue, sits there disoriented. Her eyes are cold, her face stony, exuding a baronial disdain.

"She can certainly make an impression, Ber Faytalovitsh's daughter," Gabriel thinks with pity. But nearer and dearer to him is Golde, who is now standing, caring and sympathetic, next to Ruzhke, her eyes all warmth and caresses.

Yisrultshe Blimeles trembles over Ber. His face wrinkles like a washboard.

"Ber, you were so ambitious. Was it worth it? Was it? *What profit hath a man of all his labor*? All is *vanity of vanities*." [59]

He steps over to the door, his face toward the corpse.

The two dripping candles are spattering tallow. Grunem and Itshe Tshap the letter writer are keeping vigil. Ruzhke is seated apart from them, off to the side. She never takes her eyes off the piece of bread and salt lying on the black cloth.

29

GABRIEL WON'T GET MARRIED

A pile of newspapers grows on the nailed-together boards in the corner of Gabriel's room. They lie there with fresh creases, unopened, unstained, as if hot off the press. Why spoil the loveliness of these summer days? The newspapers are laid out spitefully, facing up. Gabriel steals furtive glances at the shiny bold headlines like a drunk pining for the hard stuff.

"Self-torture," Gabriel thinks, taking a damp rag and covering the newspapers so the bold, shameless print wouldn't intrude on his little world.

What does the news from Abyssinia matter to him? What does Spain matter to him? Or China? When he still hasn't come to grips with the soldiers' cemetery in Smolin, which keeps demanding a resolution. Smolin itself is a living newspaper, which is enough for a lifetime.

On that Sabbath morning, as the people of Smolin squabbled over *aliyes* in the synagogue, the wind knocked the market stalls to pieces. In five minutes the boards had been scattered like woodchips. *Chronicle*: For three days Ber Faytalovitsh ran around the town screaming "Mora-, mora-, moratorium . . ." On the fourth day they took his rigid body down from the hook. Shloymele, Khashe's boy, poisoned himself accidentally when, driven by hunger, he ate wild chestnuts and his stomach had to be pumped. *Curiosities*: Baltshe, the rabbi's daughter, with the freckles on her face and the hunched shoulder, interpreted dreams and discovered all sorts of complexes among the Jews of Smolin. But in Gabriel's doctorly opinion it wouldn't last much longer. She couldn't live with such a Freudomania.

But enough of Smolin. What use are newspapers to Gabriel? *Jews reproduce too much*, argue their enemies. Good. He, Gabriel, would not get married. But what would become of Grunem's six children who are growing up with empty bowls? No place to be seen for them at all. What would become of Golde? Every evening that fat Yisrultshe Blimeles comes to seek his advice. He brings commendatory notes with him, all written in an ornate hand. Notes from Kernezie, from Ryczywół, from Little Mazurka, from Greater Podlasze, from who knows where else, Hotzenplotz even.[60]

"You," he says to Gabriel, "are au courant. You know what's what, who's worth something and who isn't. So should I marry her off to that lad from Kernezie?"

He furrows his brow.

"That one's studying slaughtering. It's the same story all over again. I don't know what the outlook will be for slaughtering in a year, whether one would be able to support a wife and children on that. As for the proposal from Ryczywół, he's an ordained rabbi. But they say that even with a rabbinical certification one still has to go serve in the military. Khone Baker's got a quiet boy, comes back with a new decree: mechanical ovens. Got to get rid of the old oven and install a new one, made with ceramic tiles. So I complain to Shmuel: Go ahead, take her, make a match with Golde. The sooner the better. You don't know how things'll look in a year, or where you'll stand in half a year. Gabriel, am I right or not?"

Gabriel is silent. How could he respond when all he wants is to bite and scream from anger?! He quietly grits his teeth. A sea of bitterness has accumulated within him from the newspaper headlines. Gabriel feels that this is not hostility. It's something worse: people despise him. Yisrultshe Blimeles, however, doesn't want to know about any of it. He has to go on spinning his life's thread, which he had begun in his youth. He wouldn't change the way people demanded.

Yisrultshe sits, stubbornly leaning on his walking stick. His wrinkled brow is dark, as dark as a clay dish. What consolation is there for Yisrultshe if not a pinch of snuff? He sneezes with gusto out the open window. That robust sneeze attracts Hersh Lustik's attention from the orchardist's little courtyard. He walks across the courtyard with measured strides, as if over his own estate, his eagle's brows raised high and his nostrils opened wide, as he sings to himself: *La-di-dum-dum-dum, la-di-dum-dum-dum.*

He leans through the window, takes a pinch of tobacco from Yisrultshe Blimeles' open snuffbox, and screws up his left eye.

"Why are you sitting like that, Yisrultshe, with such a sour face, and in a doctor's room?"

He fixes his black, mocking eyes on Gabriel.

"These modern doctors spread such gloom across the world." Yisrultshe shakes his head defiantly.

"And so what if he's a doctor? Does he have a Tatar's heart? Gabriel feels the Exile exactly like the rest of us. The times, the times. If one is forbidden to speak, one has to lean all the more on what's inside."

Hersh strokes his beard.

"My tooth—if you catch my meaning, Yisrultshe—is aching today. So I go around and think: 'You should be happy, Hersh, that your belly doesn't hurt. How nice for you, Hersh, that your lungs are in good shape. Praise God, Hersh, that you have a healthy heart.' After all, you know, *Panie* Gabriel, from all your doctor-learning, that a man has *ramakh eyvrim*—248 organs. When one organ hurts . . ."[61]

"But Hersh, that pain radiates through the whole body. When the wave overtakes us, we drown."

Yisrultshe Blimeles groans.

"You lower your head, Yisrultshe, till the wave passes. *Gam zeh ya'avoyr*, Yisrultshe. 'This too shall pass.' It's no trick to cry when you're slapped. Let's laugh instead, Yisrultshe. Let's receive our slaps and laugh."

Gabriel soaks up every word of Hersh's. It's as if a balm has been poured on his wounds. When Gabriel hears wise words it puts him in a good mood and makes him feel like telling jokes.

"Hersh, are you familiar with Professor Adler? He interprets everything positively. According to his school of thought the crooked always comes out straight."

Hersh shrugs his shoulders.

"I'm not a great admirer of professors, Doctor Gabriel. The best professor for a Jew is his suffering. Buck up, Yisrultshe. Make the best of the little that's given you in God's world."

Yisrultshe's shoulders squirm as he withdraws into himself.

"So what's to become of me, Hersh? I've played out my part. Grunem, my son-in-law—they've sealed up his kasha mill again. I've got a grandchild to marry off. It's difficult to find a respectable match these days. Nothing's as it should be."

"Marry her to a craftsman."

"Sure, sure," Yisrultshe shakes his head. "Getting humbler all the time. Still, he's not doing *so* badly, that son-in-law of mine, Shmuel. He can still indulge in something significant. That significant thing is what I'm looking for."

Hersh casts a searching look at Gabriel.

"Marry her to a doctor, Yisrultshe. After all, then you'd have a doctor in the family."

Yisrultshe Blimeles pricks up his ears.

"Eh? What's that? What did you say? Where'd you get that idea?"

He looks around Gabriel's room, strewn with books and packed with little bottles of medicine.

From the other side of the wall comes the sad sounds from Ber Faytalovitsh's place.

"A doctor you said, Hersh? A doctor? The idea never occurred to me."

Hersh doesn't hear him. He turns back onto the road to Cyncymin, heading to the orchard to keep watch.

30

THE TOWNSFOLK GO IN
SEARCH OF A MEANS
OF SUBSISTENCE

Apart from Cyncymin, there is still a wide open world for the people of Smolin. In the summertime the town looks like an inn. People only stay the night before moving on. But from day to day it draws closer together rather than further apart. People keep trudging together over the same sand, but they never stop travelling. Everyone is travelling. Poor people from Cobbler Street as well as the burghers whom the papers still call "bourgeois." Apart from the name *burghers* they own nothing. They strike out like birds from their nests in search of food. But the sand around Smolin couldn't feed anyone. It scorches the footsteps of the townsfolk. They pay it no heed and travel on. Smolin travels to Boża Wola and Boża Wola travels to Smolin. People travel on wagons as well as on foot, even though they know very well that there are buses now, and not too much further there's also a train. If you ask a Smoliner why he's walking, at first he'd be too embarrassed to answer. But then he'd come around and shake his head dismissively.

"It's no misfortune. One can go just as well without a train. In point of fact, it's healthier to walk."

Others joke about it.

"What's the hurry? My boats are going to sink?"

There are many things in the town which the people of Smolin could do without. They could do without the radio loudspeakers in the home of every Smolin official. They could do without the baths that the municipal authorities had constructed. Even the young people, who have tried to move heaven and earth to introduce a new order in Smolin, could also do without a book from the library—the library that they had spent eighteen years saving for and which got located in some cellar. The people of Smolin, who had been able to experience what this world has to offer for only such a short time, have once again returned to providing for their modest needs. A Smoliner learns to live on a zloty a day, a half a zloty a day, or even nothing at all. As in all things, whether dressing, or eating, or going for a walk (only in certain streets), there are two Smolins.

As a result, it has grown quieter in the marketplaces. The fairs are starting up again, but people aren't putting much energy into them. They sit calmly in their stalls, swapping memories of fairs from years past.

With the dollars that Bertshik received from his new bride (she has a brother in America), he has gotten himself a harness for the horses. Now he could drive the Smolin merchants from fair to fair. People envy Bertshik for his dollars. *But each one of us,* the townsfolk think, *used to have dollars . . .*

Bertshik sits there on his wagon like some philosopher. He has learned how to be silent. The six months he spent in the prison in Płock had given him blue rings under his eyes. He has gotten used to keeping his hands to himself, even when he feels like slapping someone. Bertshik Shmatte is gone; he is no longer given to violence. That is to say, he is no longer Bertshik. He keeps silent when the town dogcatcher doesn't want to make room for his wagon on the road and starts cursing him:

"Jew mug! Bad seed!"

Bertshik bites his lip and keeps quiet. Because he knows very well that if he but lets the steam out of his mouth it would be back to Płock for him in a heartbeat. So Bertshik has learned how not to respond even though it goes against his nature. People are amazed; not the same Bertshik at all. Bertshik has become meek, a hidden saint.

Even now, as Harshl the bookmaker is taking shoes to the fair in Little Biała and mutters behind Bertshik's back that cholera could have stricken Bertshik and Tsvetl before he'd have believed it . . .—then, too, Bertshik keeps quiet. He remembers the blows he had received from Harshl in the synagogue when Tsvetl had become a mother and Harshl was there to celebrate the circumcision. Harshl had been a chaste young man up to the wedding, so it galled him that Tsvetl had been with others. He, Bertshik, who had eaten bread from more than one oven, laughed at such things. After all, someone had to be the first. But Harshl the stitcher was very much nettled and couldn't swallow the fact that that's how it was with Tsvetl before the wedding. A man has only to think about what was . . . *No*—rueful thoughts take hold of Bertshik—*Tsvetl would not have had a good life with me* . . .

Harshl is sitting behind him. Any moment he could stab a knife into his side. It's a good thing that Grunem just then comes walking along the path, holding his boots in his hand and trudging through the sand. Bertshik stops to pick him up. He stops for quite some time as Grunem stands there, waving his hands to indicate that Bertshik should keep waiting. So Bertshik barks, "Grunem, where're you going? Grunem, why're you standing there? Grunem, what're you staring at? Roll up your kapote and hurry on up into the wagon."

Grunem plucks at his naked chin, batting the idea around for a while before getting up into the wagon. Harshl the stitcher, in a fit of pique, shifts over. They all three sit in silence. Having passed the Sabbath walking limit, at roughly a mile and a half, Harshl finally bursts out, "Grunem, where are you going?"

"Me?" Grunem asks, astonished that people are thinking about him. "Where'm I going? I'm going to Cyncymin. To Hersh Lustik's orchard, to take a look at the German Witbrot's beehives."

Bertshik gives his horses the whip.

"Move it, you worthless carcasses! Grunem, just for my sake could you go to Wyszogród instead? I'm not gonna buy extra oats on account of you."

Grunem sits lost in thought, his eyes wandering from one side of the path to the other. He sees a different world in front of him. German colonists watering their strawberries. Tomato stalks winding their way up wooden stakes. German women weeding the cauliflower beds. Grunem imagines that this field is his own. Khashe and the children wandering among the grasses, digging up potatoes, pulling up carrots, gathering bunches of beets. And if Khashe had no more than one eye—would she not be able to see how to do the work? And there's Shloymele, even though his only son, taking his plowshare to the field. Wednesday mornings harnessing the horses. He has a wagon—no, *two* wagons. He drives into town to sell his goods at the market, just like the German colonists. In the evening he drives back home to his house in the village, laying himself down to sleep beneath a linden tree. The lindens are fragrant. As he sleeps, the tree's blossoms drift down over him like downy snow.

A warmth spreads over Grunem's limbs. He dozes off. But he's unable to sleep for long. Going over the cobblestones throws him from his seat. A cart full of slaughtered swine clatters by. Smolin's gentile butcher, Kowalczyk, is heading home from the slaughterhouse. The wind fans his bloodied white apron, inflating it like a red bladder. He sticks out a glinting gold tooth and starts mocking Bertshik's horses.

"Żydowski szkapi! Jewish jades!"

The horses, unused to the lashes of a butcher, struggle against the wagon shaft and turn into the ditch. Bertshik restrains the horses. He doesn't respond to the butcher, doesn't even look in his direction. Which infuriates Kowalczyk. He clenches his fists and hisses something that makes Bertshik's blood run cold. But Bertshik doesn't budge, keeping his hands to himself and thinking about the fact that in this world there were two kinds of justice. One justice for him, Bertshik, and another for Kowalczyk the butcher.

Grunem spies a wide meadow. Peasant boys are watering cows and herding flocks of geese. In the middle of the meadow there is a large pond full of fish. Grunem imagines his little daughters watering the flocks of geese, Shloymele herding the cows, and himself driving a load of feathers to the fair in Grójec.

"Once again," Grunem says to himself out loud as Harshl the stitcher turns his head of disheveled red hair. "Once again my fantasies . . ."

Grunem knows he's sinning when he imagines fictional things as if they were real. He enjoys it in the moment, but it could only end badly. It gets his mind all jumbled up just like when he was young, sitting in the study house, and naked women danced about in his head: Lilith, the Queen of Sheba, Bathsheba. He slept on hard benches but still had to go to immerse himself in the *mikveh* in the morning . . .[62] Then his hair had really started falling out. No, he has to be strong and drive away the fantasies. It's simply ridiculous: How had the idea of this meadow even come to him? Since when did Jews have meadows? There is one community meadow behind the cemetery, which is a real dump. All the town's refuse ends up there. Pigs frisk about, digging up the mountain of garbage, dead horses, and flayed dogs. Which reminds Grunem of the community and its councilmembers.

"A meadow," he mutters next to Bertshik. "There's a municipal meadow. Why can't the councilmembers see that it should be cleaned? Sow some tomatoes, cauliflower, plant a small orchard, set up some beehives. Strawberries. Strawberries again . . . It's going badly for the Jews. It's a rotten business when the thoughts interfere."

"Who are the thoughts interfering with, eh?" Looking at Grunem's sour face neither Bertshik nor Harshl know who it's going badly for: Grunem or the Jews. Mention of the community and the councilmembers jogs Harshl's memory. He looks Bertshik over with hostility and growls, "Piddling *maftir*s are what he covets, that mangy weasel Yosl, piddling *maftir*s! Were it not for the police I'd crack his ribs."

Bertshik keeps quiet. He knows very well that Harshl doesn't mean Yosl the councilmember, but rather himself, Bertshik. All because of Tsvetl. For every sin one is punished in *this* world.

"There's Cyncymin, Grunem. Just over there! Tell Hersh Lustik that Bertshik's waiting."

Grunem extricates himself from among Harshl the stitcher's shoes and tosses off a "thanks!" at Bertshik.

"Yosl should want to be a councilmember as much as I want to go to the German to learn how to make honey."

"There are worse things than making honey. Believe me, there are far worse things," Harshl comforts him, not once taking his eyes off Bertshik.

Bertshik cracks his whip and turns onto the Wyszogród road. Now the two of them are alone together. Both keep stubbornly quiet as Tsvetl's secret hovers between them.

31

TSVETL'S PUNISHMENT

There is an epidemic in town. Scarlet fever is on the march. Not a single house escapes. Little babes pass from the world, and in Boża Wola a young mother is cut down in the prime of life. Hersh Lustik's home is full of people, coming and going. They look him in the eye as they listen to what he has to say. Soreh-Gitl, in her Turkish shawl, tears at his lapel.

"Hersh, my guardian! Why are you silent? Why aren't you out there? Why aren't you running around? Tsvetl's child is dying. My poor little grandchild. After all, Hersh, you're on the community council. Go, do everything you can!"

Ratse pinches herself on the cheeks. She was there when Tsvetl's child was born. She soothes her husband.

"Go, go now, my darling Hersh. See to saving as many as you can. He was delivered with forceps. Can we now just watch as the child dies?"

Lazar Kurnik picks at his straw-colored beard. "Quite right. You've got to see about doing something to stop this epidemic. You're a councilmember, after all."

Hersh shakes his head. "You're a sly one. I could do without this council membership. Let me go around town and see how bad the epidemic is."

He flees the house. A troop of people trudges along after him. The orchard courtyard is left empty.

Between afternoon and evening prayers the synagogue is filled with lamentations. A gang of women barges in with the force of men. In the lead comes Soreh-Gitl, wagging a thin, menacing finger.

"Khone Baker's daughter-in-law was stricken so suddenly and you menfolk just keep silent? A fire's raging in town; an epidemic snatching away infants. Incompetents and good-for-nothings, just reciting Psalms and all of a dither! Harshl, are you a father or aren't you? Why are you just standing there like a lummox?"

She runs up to the ark and throws herself down on the ground, banging her head against the steps. Harshl the stitcher is in no hurry. On his short, bear-like legs he walks over to his mother-in-law, lifts her off the ground, and sits her down on a bench.

The darkness fades from Harshl's face. His eyes lose their stubborn, steely look. Now they are gentle and mild. Even his disheveled red hair is not as frightening as before. After what happened in Little Ostra and at the fairs in Greater Podlasze, Harshl has come to understand that there would be many more misfortunes in the world. Man, Harshl realizes, has lost everything valuable. The smallest plank of a fence is more secure than man. In the face of all of this, what happened between Tsvetl and Bertshik seems utterly meaningless. Until then he had devoted all of his thoughts to what was crudely material. Never saw anything higher. Now the veil has been lifted from his eyes and he perceives his own fallenness: the fact that he had devoted all of his thoughts to something insignificant. So he wasn't Tsvetl's *first*! And what kind of achievement would that even have been? Dangers lurk in this world. Tsvetl's child is struggling with death. No, he'd forgive Bertshik. He'd forgive Tsvetl. What they did to him is in the past. Harshl feels his soul growing easier than if he'd been drained of a whole cask of poison.

The synagogue grows more and more crowded. Mothers arrive, and aunts and grandmothers. Lazar's heart eases. He bangs on the lectern.

"The town's got a rabbi, and yet nothing."

Every grieving heart turns toward the cobweb-riddled corner where the rabbi is standing, facing the wall. Two pointy ears poke out from under his stiff, faded hat. He stands there, thin and flat, like a stalk of grain battered by the wind. He makes his way swiftly across the synagogue and in two strides is already standing before the reading desk.

The crowd stares open-mouthed and bewildered across the dark space of the study house. The rabbi's hurried voice rolls out over the cold synagogue, piercing the walls, boring into minds, and sticking in hearts, so that each and every person feels himself guilty. Sin grows like a mountain, ever higher and higher. Soon the mountain would collapse, crushing the synagogue and the people alike.

"*Out of the mouth of babes and sucklings*[63]—for the sake of the little children we are being beaten with rods. *The Lord hath chastened me sore*[64]—God has punished us because of the wantonness that reigns in this town. People drink the gentiles' milk. Beds are not moved apart but rather pushed together, a thing unheard of among Jews. There is no unity. Election slates are invalidated. A dispute with the councilmembers. Denunciations. Jews are like a broom: As long as the twigs stick together, then . . ."

Hersh Lustik stands up before his lectern.

"A broom, Rabbi, doesn't make for a pleasant comparison. Better a *lulav*. A *lulav* that everyone shakes. Whoever has a hand gets to shake that *lulav* . . ."[65]

"A dried *lulav*," concedes the rabbi with his sallow, shriveled face. "Modesty is a thing of the past. Husband and wife are desecrating the commandment to be fruitful and multiply with bizarre things that are forbidden. It is the case that Jews are, God forbid, ceasing to multiply."

Yosl, the councilmember, pats his well-fed belly, his fat eyes brimming with authority. His voice comes out swollen, mon-eyed, bourgeois.

"What's her name, that dissolute girl who acted the harlot? Volf's daughter?"

Harshl the stitcher stands there with an unburdened face, ready to forgive all and everyone. His heart is full of compassion for Tsvetl. But that odious councilman, Yosl Katazhan, has in-sulted his wife, whom he had married according to the law of Moses and Israel. His sallow, overgrown face darkens again as his eyes turn to look poisonously toward Yosl. The rabbi sees that a quarrel is brewing, so he interposes himself between the two sides.

"One is not permitted to speak ill of Jewish women. But one should not be punished by speaking. What is going on among us in town? Young men and girls, they go and go, and keep going . . ."

Hersh Lustik moves closer to his lectern.

"What does it matter to you, Rabbi, if they go? Let them go. Let them not stop. Just let them go."

The mood turns melancholy. But smiles begin cropping up on their pale faces. If Hersh Lustik could joke at a time like this it's a sign that the epidemic couldn't last much longer.

The rabbi's *tallis* falls off his shoulder again, and as he puts it back he groans, "At a time such as this, when enemies arise to destroy us, we slaughter in a ritually improper way. Our butch-ers do not remove the prohibited pieces in the appropriate way. Our women are careless in the performance of their ritual obli-gations. The synagogue is frequently empty, and the young folk make a farce of everything with their wantonness and frivolity. *Let us search our ways*[66]—let us seek out our sins for we have strayed from the Jewish path."

The women stand by the door, sobbing. But Avreml "Treyf" outyells all of them. Pain cries out of him. Because he is respon-sible for supporting a wife and children.

"Rabbi!" he bellows like an ox. "I've also got a paralyzed mother that I need to care for. Go lecture the rich folk on morals!

Shmuel Łoyvitsher eats before prayers. He's got a weak heart, the glutton. All Jews seem to have weak hearts these days. When he goes to Płock he runs off to the tavern with that weak heart of his to see Zelde. Go lecture him, Rabbi. And Yosl, that councilman of ours, that skirt chaser, that bum, that ex-con, that . . . I need to live, Rabbi. Am I gonna risk it all with God for the sake of kosherness? If that's what He wanted, that's what He's got."

Bertshik Shmatte is no longer his former self. "Płock clobbered him," his "mates" say, shaking their heads. Indeed, it had wreaked havoc on the young man. But be that as it may, through all the misery and suffering, he is still Bertshik Shmatte. Bertshik who hates those respectable Jews with their false piety. Now he's sticking up for Avreml.

"Rabbi, why are you making such a fuss about Jewishness? I start dealing in bones and it's 'no more bones.' I start going to the village and it's 'no more selling in the village.' Two broken ribs and a black eye. Seems like that'd be enough. So I get a harness for the horses and start going to the fairs, then the fairs stop again. So I ask you, respectable Jews—may you get your '*His breath goeth forth*'s' [67]—what good's that Jewishness to me?"

Yisrultshe Blimeles grabs his head.

"Woe to the ears that have to hear such things! God, look what you've driven us to. Jews profaning your sacred name in a holy place. Let the war of Gog and Magog finally come! It'll last a year and then let there be an *end* to it!"

Hersh Lustik pinches him on the sleeve.

"Leave it alone, Yisrultshe. Do they even know what they're saying? It's just the misery talking. Women, go home and cook supper! And you, menfolk, come with me. Let's go and drive this plague away. Let's get bottles of rubbing alcohol, let's go from house to house, let's . . ."

The crowd tears themselves from their seats. But they halt instantly, as if paralyzed. There in the doorway of the study house stands Tsvetl, half naked, her hair loose and her eyes protruding. Two rows of white teeth, wide and sharp, glitter in the gloom. People back away in terror towards the ark. Tsvetl stands there for some time. Then she starts making her way through the men. She walks boldly and shamelessly with bare, outstretched arms. All of a sudden she tears the blouse completely from her body. Fresh, white flesh springs forth as a rasping, gravelly voice wrests itself from her breast.

"Take it, you men, take my body, drink my blood. Because of you, men, my child has left this world!"

She throws herself right at Bertshik, clawing her nails at his face.

"Take that, you! You've made a woman of me!"

She lets go of Bertshik's scratched face and sits down on the ground. As she tears off the rest of her shirt she sticks her tongue out at the rabbi and laughs wildly.

"*Ha ha ha*, lunatics! Everyone's crazy. *Ha ha ha!* Ain't no God in this world! *Ha ha ha!* Men, who wants to go with me?"

Her voice breaks as if she were being shattered from within. Soon, however, she starts to keen, gut-wrenchingly, banging her fists against her temples, and falls with her bare breasts to the ground.

32

GABRIEL TAKES
REVENGE ON SMOLIN

G olde runs quickly toward the forest on little steps. Her hair is unkempt and her dress is slightly undone at the waist. Something pink and embarrassing gleams through, drawing men's gazes. On a stone at the side of the road sits Tsvetl, singing a lullaby. Golde stops for a moment to observe the rag doll that Tsvetl is hugging, reflecting on Tsvetl's fate, before continuing on without further hesitation.

She enters the forest, running quickly past the forester's hut. Frightened does follow her with goggling eyes. The deeper she goes the darker the forest becomes. Rays of sunlight slip through the canopy of trees, showing Golde the way. She leaves the trail and wanders into the forest. Her instinct prompts her: *Go further!* She's getting tired from walking, so she stops again and looks around.

Finally she notices something. Her eyes light up. On the trunk of a fallen oak sits her cousin, Gabriel Priver, absorbed in a medical book. Golde feels like a drowning person who has finally made it to shore. It's difficult for Golde to make sense of what's happening to her. So she relies completely on her cousin; whatever he wants is what would be. She would forego thinking at all. She stands there leaning on a tree and breathing heavily. Gabriel notices the sound of her breath.

"Is that you, Golde? In the middle of the day . . ."

His blood starts running fast and hot. Here is Golde, away from Smolin, delivered to his charge. Here in the solitude of the forest he feels himself her protector. What could have happened at home? What has brought Golde here to him?

He shifts over on the trunk and makes a space for Golde. She has such a narrow waist. She has on a weekday dress, the kind one just throws on in the morning. One motion and it would tumble off. Gabriel blushes at the mere idea of it. He feels that just thinking of it would defile something.

A damp heat emanates from the dense forest. Two birds are bickering in a tall birch tree. Feathers float down onto his shoulders. Gabriel shakes them off. His blood has calmed down, his thoughts have grown clearer. An inner voice is warning him: *Gabriel, this is not the dormitory. This is Smolin. Golde has a grandfather whose name is Yisrultshe Blimeles. He has already bought himself a plot in the Smolin cemetery and wants to marry off his grandchild according to the law of Moses and Israel.*

His voice has a warm tone.

"Darling, what's happened? Tell me, Golde."

He's in good spirits, happy at the victory he has won over himself, at the evil thought he has overcome.

"He's finally come. Doesn't my cousin know? He's staying at the rabbi's."

Golde, agitated over the earlier excitement caused by her state of undress, is stirring Gabriel's blood anew. His shining blue eyes suddenly darken.

"Who's staying at the rabbi's, Golde?"

"The suitor from Ryczywół!" Golde says angrily, irritated that Gabriel has taken no interest in the matter before.

Gabriel's face flushes a brilliant red, like a copper pan. But his sharp nose trembles, white. A man gets very upset when the thing he considers most sacred is affected. Smolin duped him. That Yisrultshe Blimeles, his uncle, who had spoken such tender words, could turn around and kick him. And he, Gabriel, has tended to Smolin so nobly, has treated Golde with such respect, and wanted the whole world to praise him for it. No, the people of Smolin were ungrateful people. All of a sudden it's *"Hey, here's a suitor from Ryczywół!"* From now on he would treat Smolin more harshly.

"Where is this 'suitor,' Golde? Have you seen him for yourself?"

Golde is upset.

"I *said* he was staying at the rabbi's. Baltshe says he's got a little red beard. And he's got some kind of illness. What do they call it there? A *Freudian* sickness . . ."

"A little red beard," Gabriel repeats, distracted by his thoughts.

He turns around hastily. Golde's eyes are aglow, waiting for some resolution. The leaves are giving off a hot vapor. It smells of mint. The gnats are restive, biting Gabriel with their pointy, little red beards. Heat flows through the forest, like a glowing mass. It swamps the mind, confusing one's thoughts. Golde is now quite ill at ease. Her body is translucent. Here in the forest, all of her hidden femininity is now liberated from its concealment, becoming for Gabriel so close, so undeniable, so obvious. His head feels like lead and the grasses tempt him, urging him down. Gabriel's thoughts are hiding somewhere, his clear understanding concealed.

The world has turned away from Gabriel. No more Smolin, no more Yisrultshe Blimeles, no more red-haired suitor. There is nothing but Golde. His Golde and this solitude in the forest on a hot, sultry morning.

A deep, restless anticipation is awakened in Golde, together with a sweet fear. In her impotent silence she sees Gabriel's arms, broad and familiar. Her eyes drift with a pellucid light. She sees something which comes but once in a lifetime. Like the pain of childbirth. Like the pangs of death. But it all retreats from Golde into the lostness of the moment.

33

HERSH LUSTIK
BECOMES A WIDOWER

What has become of Ratse? She is utterly unrecognizable. Day by day her dark face turns lighter and more transparent. It shines with a brightness as never before in *this* world. The bitterness of a wife who would never be a mother leaves her, evaporating completely. Her eyes, full of kindness, smile with a childlike innocence at everyone, even Tsvetl, the crazy woman who throws garbage in through her window. Ratse has at last reached an understanding with the world. She no longer harbors any grudges against anyone, nor does she demand anything from anyone—neither from people nor from God. If someone should wrong her, she would forgive him on the spot. Some bring seven children into the world and others are barren. Ratse raised others' children but did not have the honor of one of her own. Hersh, her husband, would say Kaddish for her instead. That's how it had been decreed somewhere far, far away from Smolin.

The worst thing, though, is the fact that her knees are failing. What's more, the thoughts have stopped in her mind. She seems to see everything when in fact she sees nothing at all. Ratse has ended up like a small child. That idea has a grip on her.

"Hersh!" she says, waking her husband. "Is it true that an old person and a child are the same?"

Drops of light drip through the gaps in the shutters. Hersh Lustik stretches out in bed. His eyes are closed but he's only dozing. He answers Ratse half-asleep.

"Of course they're the same, Ratse. The souls of old folk are pure, like those of children."

"Their souls, yes, Hersh. But what about their bodies? I'd rather not have sinned by complaining."

"Dear silly little fool," Hersh comforts her. "*Kol zman she-haneshomo be-kirbi*[68]—for as long as there's a soul within a person it sustains the body and makes it noble."

Ratse grimaces.

"Let's just leave that nobility alone. I'm not worthy of mentioning the good Lord because I haven't washed my hands."

She goes back to sleep. She dreams of her wedding night. She is sitting in a canopy bed bedecked with blue silk. Little rosy-faced cherubs with lips the color of bright corals are flying around the posts. They fly down to her. Right in the middle of them flies Tsvetl's child. Ratse holds the whole flock of cherubs in her lap. Her breasts flood with milk. She suckles the children. They draught on her, tugging at her nipples till she is out of breath. Nothing can pass through her throat, and her mind is an utter carnival. She wants Hersh to take the children. She stretches a hand out towards him but her hand remains stiff and unable to move. Suddenly that swarm of children flies away from her. She could breathe deeply again. She grows more at ease. She is as light as a down feather. The feather begins to fly higher and higher until it disappears into the clouds.

·:·

Hersh stands with his mouth agape. He shakes Ratse by the arm and moistens her lips with water. Ratse lies silently, her eyes set in a fixed stare. Hersh doesn't want to believe that Ratse could do such a thing to him, so he implores her, "What's gotten into you? Don't be silly Ratse. Ratse, Ratsele."

Beads of sweat like pearls break out on his smooth forehead as the blood rushes to his temples. Red wheels spin before his eyes. With the last of his energy he drags himself to the cupboard. He wants to fetch some apple juice. But his hands won't come down. He just stands there in the middle of the room.

"What's gotten into you, Ratse? This is so unexpected; I'm completely unprepared . . ."

Ratse's upper lip is curled up, her mouth twisted, but in the corners flutters the shadow of a smile. Hersh thinks he hears Ratse's voice, coming as if from a deep well that a stone had just fallen into:

"It's nothing, Hersh, it's nothing. Let the world go on doing what the world does."

He chokes on his tears. He sits down on a footstool, near Ratse's head. Sorrow weighs on his head, pushing it down to the ground.

"You'll be a lonely man now, Hersh" sorrow whispers in his ear. "Ratse has left you . . . You're all alone in the world . . ."

The sun rises over Smolin in a hot embrace. The canary twitters at him from its little cage, consoling him: "Don't surrender, Hersh. Don't give up!"

A flock of doves shuffles around the windows. They peck at the glass, boldly demanding the crumbs that Ratse had gotten them used to receiving. Hersh takes a couple of pieces of stale challah, crumbles them up, and tosses them to the doves. He is suddenly reminded of his childhood when he used to chase the doves, the grandparents of the ones he's now feeding. And Ratse's pale face keeps smiling at him.

"That's good, Hersh. The world is big and beautiful. So why shed tears?"

The sun is already high when Hersh Lustik rises from weeping over his wife. He puts on the greenish coat that in his old age he has started wearing on weekdays to give it a good dusting. He takes the silk kerchief off his neck and leaves to see about a grave for Ratse. Crushed, he leans on his tall walking stick as he walks. Ratse's words echo in his ears.

"Let the world go on doing what the world does."

He straightens his back and, with his head raised, goes in to see the head of the Jewish community.

"Shmuel, Ratse has been taken from me. So I have come to ask for a grave for my wife."

He doesn't speak again until the funeral.

34

"VA-YOMOS YOYSEF"— AND JOSEPH DIED

The radio blares from Schultz's restaurant, echoing through half the marketplace. That's how it is every evening: between afternoon and evening prayers it would announce new decrees to the people of Smolin. People would close their transom windows, shut the doors of their shops; they would put on false smiles so that their neighbors might not know what was really going on inside. The townsfolk subscribe to the principles: *Pinch your cheeks so the color stays . . . Put a brave face on it . . . If you don't behave like someone beaten, you won't get beaten . . .* They make jokes, and curse the German and his radio. It does not, however, lighten their spirits. The radio drills its way through thick walls, filling the little courtyards and pestering like an annoying fly. A lament carries out over the marketplace from one pump to the other: "*Va-yomos Yoysef*—And Joseph died. *Va-yokom melekh khodosh*—Now there arose a new king, which knew not Joseph." [69]

Gabriel Priver is reading books of moralistic literature. Two thoughts could not all of a sudden coexist peacefully. Either one had a good thought or a bad one. From the yellowed pages he hears words of comfort: *Rejoice in life, Gabriel. Understand and forgive! Then the good thoughts will overcome the bad ones.*

But such is above the abilities of man—so he hears the voice of his own blood. *Your medical arts have deceived you; psychotherapy has not been successful for you. Good manners won't help you at all. It's not up to you. Others are pushing towards that. The looks of the pastor, the mayor, the pharmacist. They speak and remind you at every turn: 'After all, you're not the same Gabriel Priver as a year ago; you're not the same as six months ago or even two weeks ago.'*

Gabriel's value as a human being is declining in his own estimation like the value of banknotes in wartime. After every speech on the radio his self-worth diminishes even further. The common stock of humanity amounts to nothing. There are really two different kinds of man. Just as the prophet Isaiah had predicted, only the reverse . . . So he implores himself: *Just agree, Gabriel, that you are living in such an atmosphere, in such a climate. That this climate is what it is and not otherwise. Conform to it, change your habits and your way of thinking according to it. How would it be, Gabriel, if you had been born into this climate and had only ever lived at such a time as you are right now, eh? That someone could be born blind?*

Gabriel is ashamed to look people in the eye. He's ashamed at the fact that they *aren't* ashamed. It irritates him that they rouse the savage within him, the wild beast that dwells within all of us. Poisonous gases are building up inside of him that threaten to burst his body open at any moment.

That won't do, someone warns him. It's the voice of the Bratslaver.[70] *Gabriel, you must find yourself a way. The conduits, as it is written, the pipes through which the poison may be released and evaporate. Your hatred, Gabriel, will not protect you. This hatred will destroy you. After all, what good is hatred without strength? You should assume that you're living before the "Declaration of the Rights of Man." You are a* Ghetto Jew! *And in any event, the people of Smolin think it's still before the French Revolution. They have always looked around for who is pursuing them.*

Gabriel feels confined between the four walls of his room. Outside, the sky is full of stars, as always, without any ulterior motive. The blue-tinted night drapes Smolin, cuddling it, caressing it, calming it. The radio loudspeaker now carries church hymns on the same frequency, full of love and forgiveness. Gabriel rubs his forehead. Didn't these thoughts bother him from time to time? Hadn't he paid good attention to them? How could the two thoughts fit? He keeps losing his way; he walks aimlessly. But his footsteps lead him from himself to his family. Everything happens in reality. His cousin Sheva is sitting in front of the store, chatting with the other women.

"You can't cook a thing in this heat."

Old Zisl walks up to him, leaning on her little cane.

"Pardon, Cousin, but the plague is over."

Khashe, her elbow bare, stands in the doorway, away from her wealthy sister. The children are playing in the rain gutter, bickering over a piece of candy.

Gabriel recovers his former good mood. Everything is as it had been. Like yesterday and the day before that. For the moment nothing in Smolin has changed. But where is Golde? It has already been three days since he last saw her. From that time in the forest . . . Golde is avoiding him. In a few steps he is in Yisrultshe Blimeles' little garden. He runs through the narrow tree-lined avenues, cutting a path among the garden beds. Golde is sitting on the bench under the oak. She's not alone. Baltshe, the rabbi's daughter, is sitting next to her, pale and hunched over. She's holding Golde's hand in hers, interpreting one of her dreams.

"Glass," she says, her eyes feverish. "Glass . . . If you dreamt you'd harmed yourself with glass, Freud says that . . . Just a moment, I'll remember . . ."

"Miss Baltshe, Freud's useless. Adler's better. Individual psychology brings a person more happiness, Miss Baltshe!" Gabriel interjects jovially.

Baltshe's face flushes. Embarrassed, she stammers, "The doctor is an amiable person. But I still won't alter my convictions. Freud is everything to me. He can explain why my will is weak, why I cannot get used to people, why I cannot play, or laugh. Freud can interpret everything for me. I am on the trail of those traits I inherited from my father. In the very midst of this work on myself I cannot cast Freud aside. But I won't keep you. Good night!"

She leaves quickly, with hurried, anxious steps. Gabriel watches as she withdraws. It seems as if her momentum spurs her on.

"She won't live long. She's stewing in her own juices. And those juices are drying up day by day," Gabriel says to Golde who is lost in thought, her eyes toward the ground as if looking for something.

The two of them sit in silence. The sweet silence of people who have voluntarily accepted a secret that keeps them apart from others. She docilely submits to Gabriel's caresses. Any resistance, any struggling is meaningless.

"Golde, what's the matter with you? You're so serious, so distracted. I want you to laugh. It's so good for me when you're cheerful."

Golde takes Gabriel's walking stick and draws something in the sand. She lifts her head slowly and scrutinizes his face, carefully inspecting every little line as if seeing him for the first time.

"I want to leave Smolin. Flee to somewhere far away."

"Why? Don't you like Smolin? How far do you want to run, Golde?"

"How can I explain it . . . Everyone walks around moaning. They all think the worst of everything. I had a terrible dream tonight."

"Golde, you want to go away and leave me behind?"

Golde blushes as if one of her hidden thoughts has been found out.

"I can't get rid of the dream."

Gabriel takes of both of her hands in his.

"Golde, you have no reason to run away. Running doesn't make anything better."

Golde snuggles into him like a child.

"I'm afraid, Gabriel. My shadow is following me longer and more strangely. I'm so frightened! Every night I dream the same thing. I die and my cousin, you, Gabriel, are following me. Baltshe says that a person can forebode what will happen to him."

Gabriel strokes her hair and pats her hands.

"Sow your dreams to the wind, Golde. Baltshe doesn't know what she's talking about. Baltshe doesn't know what it means to be happy. Baltshe lacks humor. She doesn't feel the charm of being alive. Nothing's going to happen to you, Golde. It's forbidden to happen to you. Uncle Yisrultshe intimated to me something about 'Jewishness.' For me, Golde, 'Jewishness' is not so terrifying. I look at such things differently. Golde, we'll travel a great deal, see the world. But our home will be Smolin."

Golde throws her arms around his neck. "I'm so afraid, Gabriel, I'm terrified of something. I don't even know what. Since then . . ."

Gabriel feels Golde's hot breath on his chest. He puts his lips to her hair.

"Love is within us, Golde. It doesn't depend on other people. Whoever truly loves can endure so much. Golde, don't be afraid of the time in which we live. The good within us no one can crush."

The dew descends on the fields of Smolin, coating the grass in a white gauze. Golde dozes in Gabriel's arms. Her heart beats calmly. He could feel the warm pulse of her blood.

Elsewhere on their floor a candle is lit. Yisrultshe Blimeles rises for midnight prayers.

35

MOSHKE BECOMES A
RESPECTABLE PERSON

Tsvetl lies bound in a wagon full of straw. The whole street-ful of knitters stands with their hands concealed, listening to her wild cries. Soreh-Gitl, in her worn-out wig, drags herself up onto the cart. She sits down by her daughter's head, beating her gaunt fists against her temples. Her eyes are vacant.

"What has befallen me!"

Tsvetl, exhausted from screaming, has fallen asleep like a little chicken. But as soon as Lazar Kurnik gives a lash of the whip and the cart lurches from its place she awakens with a start, turns towards the town, and starts wailing out over the marketplace.

"People, a severe decree has been issued against us. Go home, hide in your cellars, bolt your doors and chain your shutters! They're on their way, they're coming, they're already here! Where has my child disappeared? Fools, why're you just standing there? Idiots, what're you staring at?!"

Amidst Tsvetl's cries, a quiet lad with a wooden box on his shoulder slips into the marketplace. He walks like a stranger, and it's with an outsider's eyes that he observes the town. Itshe Tshap, the letter writer, sees Moshke first and calls him over to his wagon. People clear the way for him and stand around holding their breath and watching as Soreh-Gitl meets her son. Her face is stony. Her lips, stiff and bloodless, barely move. She motions her hand at Moshke.

"This is Tsvetl, your sister. I am your mother. And your father's lying in the ground."

Moshke is silent. Asks no one a thing. He takes his box with the grant of amnesty pasted on the side and sets off home.

He seldom appears among his friends. His foreignness and stubborn silence drive them away. In the evening, when the young people take walks along the sidewalks in front of the Jewish houses, people look in through the gaps in his shutters and see Moshke pouring over heavy books by the light of a little oil lamp.

From them on, when he goes out into the street he is met everywhere with looks of respect. People whisper behind his back and watch how he walks, how he holds his head, how he greets people.

"He's grown more respectable, more sensible," the well-off Jews say, nodding their heads.

"That boy's come down to earth," the mothers of marriage-able daughters piously whisper in their ears. "He treats his mother differently now."

"He knows French and English!" Moshke's friends, the brush makers, relate enviously. "Finished a Gymnasium course in prison."

"But in Smolin he'll be able to accomplish nothing with all that. Nothing . . ."

Soreh-Gitl hears the adulation of the women. Her face is stony. She shakes her head with displeasure.

"When Tsvetl recovers, I'll get to know life as an old person. But for now I'm like the peacock: when it looks at its beautiful throat it laughs; and when it looks at its ugly feet it cries."

Since Ratse died, Hersh Lustik has spent Sabbaths with Soreh-Gitl. He lets Moshke explain socialism, always thinking of Ratse, whom he was left with nothing to remember her by, and consoles Soreh-Gitl.

"One has to look at the beautiful throat, Soreh-Gitl, and not at the ugly feet. Only at the beautiful throat."

PART II

36

WHERE IS THE
TOWN SA-MA-LIN?

O ne might very well think *Sa-ma-lin* to be located somewhere in Belarus, Lithuania, or Bohemia.

Yet those who think that would be deceiving themselves,
and the author of this description would bear absolutely no
responsibility.

Sa-ma-lin is not in Lithuania, nor in Belarus, and certainly
not in Bohemia.

"Where then *is* this *Sa-ma-lin*?"

There is some dispute among scholars on this point. Some
geographers contend that *Sa-ma-lin* is located in Mexico. Others
that it is in Pennsylvania. There is also a claim that *Sa-ma-lin* lies
in the land of Ophir where they mine gold and onyx.[71] But it is the
humble conjecture of the author of this book that *Sa-ma-lin* is to be
found neither in Mexico, nor in Pennsylvania, nor indeed in
Ophir. Rather, *Sa-ma-lin* is located in China, on the river Hong-
Kong, forty-three miles southeast of the city Ku-an-fu where Jews

have lived since the time of the destruction of the First Temple. As evidence one can mention the *Sa-ma-lin* synagogue with its pyramidal, three-tiered Chinese roof, as well as the ark-curtain with its snake decorated in the Chinese style. There is yet another opinion, namely that the angel Samael had his kingdom there. That is where, so say the Chinese Jews, the name *Sa-ma-lin* originates.

Now that we know at last where *Sa-ma-lin* is located, we can conclude this description, because the author abides by Hersh Lustik's rule: If there's got to be a story, let it be a short one.

If there's something that has displeased the reader, let him neither pose any questions nor bear any resentment against the author who has already suffered enough exasperation over the whole thing.

⁓

It seems that Gabriel Priver has swum to a quiet shore. Sa-ma-lin has given him the spiritual calm that comes from having lived through the first half of one's life. The forest has drawn out of him the poisons produced while in the bowels of the big cities. The cool river air quiets his agitated senses. Fresh powers slumber within him. The older he gets the stronger he feels the zest for life. Those twelve years he had lived abroad seem to him like a chasing after shadows. Now he is once again rooted in Sa-ma-lin. He treads on solid ground.

In the morning, Golde prepares him a meal. This is no ordinary meal. The coffee pot comes from the family's old Chinese porcelain, and the saltcellar bears the stamp of Sabbath contentment. Golde flutters about the room like a warm spring breeze. She makes the bed and smoothes the pillow with maternal affection. What Gabriel had most enjoyed from his youth is what Golde now gives him. In these everyday, womanly labors Gabriel feels the real substance of life.

He gets up from the table, taking his medical bag. Golde, with the matter-of-factness of an entitled wife, reminds him of his duties.

"Someone's sick at the German Witbrot's."

"The widow Soreh-Gitl has had an attack."

"Grandpa has asked for a prescription for some pills."

Gabriel's patients have increased. His prestige in Sa-ma-lin grows along with his feeling of usefulness, which is both gratifying and buoys his esteem. His work is his protection against all insults and humiliation. He has gotten his equilibrium back.

As he leaves he kisses Golde on the lips. Her face blushes delicately.

"Mama has asked us not to be late for lunch."

Gabriel leaves the house with the warm feeling that what's behind him is a home. He is delightedly soaking up the strong sunlight flooding the bright morning in Sa-ma-lin as he thinks about his tormented friends in the cafés in the big cities in Europe. What kind of substance does their pure thinking have without action! A giant skull tottering on rickety legs.

Gabriel experiences a zest for life and feels the need to devote himself to others, to do what's necessary and good for them. Whenever his duty towards his fellow man, to those who are suffering, is roused within him, his soul feels purified and exalted. A warm wave of love rushes through his blood. Every single person he encounters he is eager to shake hands with, to be gladdened by his joy.

As if to accommodate this wish, the Chinese knacker's boy comes running by, mysteriously distressed. Just three days earlier Gabriel had resuscitated him when he was pulled half-drowned from the Yellow River. The old knacker shook his queue, expressing his concern over a coffin for his son: "You saved Chan-Khai a worry, Mr. Doctor!" he had said, kissing Gabriel's hand for having saved his son.

Now Gabriel good-humoredly calls the little boy over to him.

"Sa-ta-shek, Sa-ta-shek, come here, show me your wounded knee."

Sa-ta-shek looks at him sidelong, hostile and obstinate. He sniffs through his round little nose and squints his diminutive Chinese eyes as he tosses aside his queue, hanging like a cat's tail.

"Do you want something, Sa-ta-shek?"

"I want everything; everything's what I want," Sa-ta-shek answers like a spoiled child and jumps up in his little Chinese shoes. As he dashes off he suddenly remembers something. He clenches his fists threateningly at Gabriel, "Jew, Jew, Jew!"

Gabriel feels like laughing at the earnest expression on Sa-ta-shek's face and his soot-blackened nose. But the humidity that always precedes a typhoon saps him of the desire to laugh.

It suddenly occurs to him that it's been three days since old Ma-ta-sha, his maid, has been to clean his room and that as a result all the work has fallen to Golde. *What's going on with this ever-obedient and good-natured Chinese woman, Ma-ta-sha?*

The street comes to an end at last. Gabriel stands at the intersection, remembering that it's Thursday, the day when the Chinese bring rice to the marketplace and Sa-ma-lin prepares food for the Sabbath. The marketplace, however, is empty, every door shut and window shuttered. The Jewish booths stand submissive and obsequious before the pagoda. Sa-ma-lin is holding its breath.

A vagrant dog hobbles across the street and sniffs the cobblestones. It stops in front of Avreml's butcher shop, menacing its claws at the shut door. It scratches stubbornly and angrily for a long time until it finally succeeds in scraping something out through the slight opening. Gripping the bone between its teeth it disappears into Yisrultshe Blimeles' courtyard.

All alone, Gabriel strolls the streets of Sa-ma-lin. He's looking for the usual, weekday boisterousness that he has finally gotten used to. But Sa-ma-lin has become too static. The unnatural quiet is beginning to unsettle him.

From out of nowhere a horse appears without a coachman. Its tail tied up in a large knot, it walks reluctantly over to the pump and looks around with unyielding eyes. It sticks out a long, thirsty tongue and remains there with its empty cart, helpless and alone in its equinity. At the other end of the street a "coolie" appears, his thin queue hanging down. Gabriel is thrilled. Finally a person. He raises a hand, but the coolie is in a hurry, apparently on some kind of errand.

The Japanese restaurant is full of coolies. Gruff, drunken voices spill into the marketplace. In the dryness of the air Gabriel senses the imminence of the typhoon. This foreboding rises in him until it transforms into actual terror.

Just like when one has a dream and wants to convince one's sleeping self that it's only a dream, so Gabriel goes from one courtyard to another knocking on the doors of all his patients. No one opens up for him. He feels the walls. This is *not* a dream. His senses are alert. A pair of grey eyes appear suddenly in a dormer window and then disappear again. They have to have been Grunem's eyes. But how have they gotten up to the roof when Grunem lives below? All at once Gabriel is seized by the desire to rush to the alarm bell and ring it, to wake up everyone up and alert them that the typhoon is approaching.

Gabriel feels the danger with all of his senses. And amidst all that apprehension it hits him like a blow to the head: Golde.

He turns back round through the marketplace. In the doorway of the Japanese restaurant barefoot coolies, beltless and with long queues, are gathering. Chinese women with blushing faces shuffle past him. Striding out in front is Ma-ta-sha, his maid! Her nostrils are flared wide, her pitted face shining. Gabriel is astounded at her strength. This old woman has been utterly reinvigorated. But in all the confusion she hasn't seen him. She just keeps giving orders:

"To Sha-ma-lei! To Sha-ma-lei!"

The typhoon steadily approaches. Young saplings groan in the wind. Hail pelts the windows. Dogs all over town begin to howl. Gabriel's body is soaked in a cold sweat. He wants to find a place to be safe from the typhoon. But everywhere is locked up. Every door shut and window shuttered. The walls are mute, as are the stones. He himself is also mute. Mute. Mute — — — — — —

The storm spurs him on; he starts running. At last he reaches his house. The typhoon has thrown Ber Faytalovitsh's piano out into the street. The wind is moving its keys. Sa-ma-lin's white-washed cobblestones groan. As if Ruzhke's final sighs.

A disaster has befallen Gabriel's house—everything's destroyed. He walks on glass, trips over pieces of furniture, gets tangled up in a quilted blanket. He feels a burning sensation. He puts his hand to his cheek, smearing his face with blood and feathers. Only with great effort is he able to make a path through the mountain of debris.

A heap of books has been tossed into the middle of the room. Broken pieces of medical equipment are strewn about in the corners. The bed, which Golde had made not long before, lies with its head facing down and its foot up in the air. All the familiar warmth which Gabriel had dreamed of is gone from that bed. It looks like a four-legged creature stricken lame. The smell of camphor and ether waft across the room and sting his eyes. His voice trembles.

"Golde! Golde!"

Only his echo replies in the half-empty room.

With his feet he pushes the overturned chairs out of the way and heads into the kitchen. Here, in Ma-ta-sha's domestic realm, everything is in its proper place. But a painful silence has settled over all the neatly arranged plates and containers. Everything breathes the mute fear which the typhoon had cast over everyone. Gabriel spies a disheveled head of hear half-concealed behind the coal bin. Golde's face is petrified with terror. The corners of her mouth are twisted in a grimace. A large green fly is licking the foam from her lips. Gabriel takes hold of Golde by her bare, blackened arms. His eyes swell with blood.

"Golde, Golde. Why are you silent, Golde?"

Something painful and sharp rises in Gabriel's mind, as if someone were thrusting a spear into his heart. He rips the blouse from Golde's body. Two firm, round little breasts with rosy nipples stare out at him, bold and resolute. Golde is not ashamed. She doesn't even lower her eyes.

Gabriel puts his ear to her breasts. He listens and listens, but he hears nothing but the pulse in his own temples——————

37

GABRIEL REMAINS IN SA-MA-LIN

They carry Yisrultshe Blimeles' coffin forth, draped in a *tallis*. It's before sunrise. The martkeplace, scrubbed clean of glass, teems with people. The corpse has brought the people of Sa-ma-lin out of their houses and restored their courage. They follow the cortège undaunted. That's who they are. After all, they have nothing left to lose, except their naked lives.

Old Zisl with her pale face unpowdered for three days, takes her little cane and makes a path for herself through the men.

"Excuse me, allow me through to my husband, to Yisrultshe."

The men make two lines to let her pass. She breathes heavily. Her wig is askew and one could see half of her short-cropped head. The three days of havoc which the typhoon had wreaked on Sa-ma-lin have caused Zisl to lose her elegance. Now she is an old, eighty-three year-old Sa-ma-lin Jewish woman. She grabs hold of a fringe dangling from her husband's *tallis* and doesn't let go.

"And who could have expected this? Such a *Jew*! Such a Jew."

Lazar Kurnik slaps his hands together. At every step he leans on his cane, because his sides are no longer so straight anymore.

Hersh Lustik, with one of his eyes stuck shut and wearing a tall turban twisted in several tiers on his head, looks like an Indian maharajah. His open eye, the right one, shoots sparks. He is looking around in every direction in search of the mandarin in charge of the town. But it's still early. Respectable Brahmins are still asleep. Only a couple of coolies are waiting in the doorway of the Japanese restaurant. They are wearing new shoes. In their vests golden chains glint in the bluish pre-dawn light. Some of them mock the cortège. These Chinese mimic blind Khashe as she mourns her father.

"Hay-vay, ta-ta-lo, ta-ta-lo!" [72]

Old Zisl has little strength to follow her husband's cortège. She stops frequently to catch her breath. She casts her rebukes aimlessly into the world.

"Excuse me, what's all the rush? Yesterday, you'll forgive me, and the day before that, and the day before the day before that, when the tempest came, no one was in such a hurry."

Behind Yisrultshe Blimeles a second corpse is being carried, escorted by the Sa-ma-lin coachmen and rag dealers. During the three days of the great storm the cemetery was abandoned. The hearse had gone missing somewhere, with its wheels and axles. Only the coffin had been found lying smashed in a ditch across from the knacker Chan-Khai's hut. Now Bertshik Shmatte is being carried, wrapped in a black shawl.

"His body was riddled with holes like a sieve."

Avreml "Treyf" shakes his weary head.

"My father-in-law was clearly an honest Jew. But Bertshik was a saint. He risked his life during the tempest."

Grunem groans. Contained in that groan is the Schadenfreude of someone who feels he was right all along; that what he predicted had come to pass.

Harshl the stitcher keeps asking Bertshik's forgiveness. Apart from a couple of blows in the synagogue, Harshl had never harmed Bertshik. But what Harshl had wished of Bertshik, since his wedding, should only happen to a mad dog.

From off in the distance Tsvetl comes running. Her hospital gown is as stiff as a board and as dark as the cheap, coarse-meal bread that Khone Baker baked. Two tight braids dangle down her shoulder. She shouts after the cortège, "Bertshik Shmatte! Three and sixteen a ticket . . . Go off and get a job as a servant . . ."

She sticks out a long tongue at her husband, Harshl, and lifts up her shirt right in front of the men.

They turn their heads away and return to remembering Bertshik. Grunem looks at Hersh Lustik. His eyes blink at the black shawl enwrapping Bertshik.

"Look what kind of resistance we put up!"

Hersh Lustik nods his tall turban and responds wordlessly, *In any event, a man doesn't live forever.*

"Fear did this to Yisrultshe, fear," Zisl says, banging her cane against the cobblestones. "Just think about it: a man with a weak heart stays in the attic for forty-eight hours without anything to eat. The rats never let him close an eye. And with, you'll excuse me, a dead cat to boot."

Golde is carried last, thirty paces behind her grandfather. The narrow black cloth puts the contours of her body into sharp relief, the roundness of her arms and her long neck.

Shmuel follows his daughter with an unfamiliar gait. He is ashamed to look people in the eye and holds his head hanging down. Shmuel knows very well that he is walking on stones, on the Sa-ma-lin cobbles. But he sees something quite different before his eyes.

He sees the old, broken chair on which the heads of the Sa-ma-lin community had sat for hundreds of years. He sees bits of silk from his dry goods store fluttering about, the store that his great-grandfather had opened in Sa-ma-lin. The only thing he truly sees, however, is Golde, his only daughter, being carried on two simple, hastily nailed-together boards.

And here is Sheva, Golde's mother. She's no longer tall. Three days had shriveled her body, rendering it unrecognizable. Her once lively, moist eyes are now dry, as if their sparkle had disappeared. Her lips are blue. Her voice sounds wooden.

"Such a blooming rose. Just look, people, at what has befallen me. Take a look at this black wedding!"

Khashe makes a sign of agreement with her good eye at Sheva.

"Both of us have met with a grim misfortune! Our lone, poor father."

In Khashe's misery lies the bitter consolation that this death has finally reconciled the two sisters.

The burghers of Sa-ma-lin speak little. But that silence, joined with the sight of the black cavities of the broken windows, chills the blood in their veins.

The tempest that had rampaged across Sa-ma-lin for three days died down. Nothing is left concealed; everything has been uncovered. People finally know who has removed their shame. What people had once thought and felt is now over and done with. But after such painful contact, people are brought closer together. People have finally come to an agreement. Tomorrow they would again live in peace.

Gabriel walks among that crowd of Jews like a stranger. What's his relation to these people? Their black beards now terrify him with the distance of passing time. He had wanted to kindle within himself the feeling of family and had come to Sa-ma-lin. He came here to collect on his childhood and to settle a debt. But what is Sa-ma-lin? Two hundred crooked, dilapidated shacks that need to be torn down. Sickly Jews, nourished on onions and garlic just like their grandfathers and great-grandfathers before them. What does he, Gabriel Priver, a doctor and a European, have to do with them? Staying in Sa-ma-lin no longer makes any sense.

A breeze blows in off the river. It plays mischievously with the black cloth covering Golde. The pinky of her right foot is uncovered; the glint from her toenail blinds Gabriel. Golde! Soon the yellow earth of Sa-ma-lin would cover her completely. This Sa-ma-lin earth . . . It draws things to it . . .

Someday it would cover Gabriel, too. How could he now go away from Sa-ma-lin and leave Golde behind? Why only Golde? Who would heal the wounds of the people of Sa-ma-lin? When the foreign doctor—the one they took for a gentile—is among them they feel more secure. No, there is no other recourse for him. His fate is bound to the earth of Sa-ma-lin. He would like for Golde to know that. But Golde remains silent, and now she is carrying off the secret, their secret, into eternity.

They avoid the last houses. Beyond the town the cortège stretches out like a long, black stain on the yellow road. Now their hearts are freer, less restrained. Their sighs dissipate unhindered across the rice paddies of China, echoing in the metallic rustle of the leaves in the trees. Sa-ma-lin has carried the pain from its cramped houses and cries that pain out to the heavens.

The abandoned crowd, forgotten by the world, draws closer and closer to the cemetery. Fresh, thirsty tears cling to the cold stones.

But this time the headstones could not ease their pain. The headstones themselves need consoling. The typhoon had deformed and broken them. They are strewn across the turned-over mounds of dirt. The gate, torn from its hinges, was carried off somewhere by the storm. The people of Sa-ma-lin think nothing of themselves and begin wailing over the destruction wrought upon their ancestors and their graves.

The mound over Yisrultshe Blimeles' grave grows steadily higher. Each person pours on another shovelful of yellow sand to lighten the burden on their heavy hearts. New wellsprings of energy surge up in Gabriel. The louder the drumming of the dirt the stronger the force growing within him. Coldly, with a stony heart and clenched teeth, he ministers to Khashe.

"Dear people, have pity! The bright light has suddenly been taken from me. Grunem, where are you, Grunem? My good eye has gone out. A dark night, people. Darling father! I saw you for the last time in your grave and I will never see you again. And who will wash you, my living orphans?"

Khashe is led away from her father's grave. She stretches out her long, poorly nourished face and gropes her hands forward, completely blind at last.

Misfortune has befallen Sheva twofold. She stands by her father's grave and does not take her eyes off Golde, who lies so modestly upon the two boards waiting for her proper burial. Sheva doesn't know which to weep over first. In her grief she faints into the arms of her cousin, the doctor Gabriel Priver.

Nearer the fence they are lowering Bertshik Shmatte into his grave. Here the village produce sellers and a couple of his friends from the shuttered library are making a fuss. Harshl the stitcher bends over. He asks Bertshik for forgiveness for the last time.

"For those blows that time in the synagogue . . ."

Avreml "Treyf" shouts into the grave, "You were a good friend in this life, Bertshik. May it not be otherwise in the next. May you demand justice everywhere. The devil take your . . ."

From atop the wall mad Tsvetl bursts into loud laughter, clapping her hands.

Old Zisl, her elbows jutting out like wings, shoves her way through the men.

"Excuse me, menfolk, let me through to see my husband. Snatched away so suddenly. Hadn't even run out of pills."

Yellow leaves scatter over Yisrultshe Blimeles' grave. The wind plays with the people's long coattails and casts their firm booming voices across the ripe rice paddies:

"*Yis-ga-dal ve-yis-ka-dash.*" [73]

Hersh Lustik extricates himself from a small group of people. He bends over the grave. Each of his words falls like a drop of dew upon the sore hearts of the people of Sa-ma-lin.

"I am letting you know, Yisrultshe, that this town will be rebuilt. I, Hersh Lustik, will stand surety for that."

His face burns with courage in the red light of the rising sun.

NOTES

Chapter 1

1 *Counting of the Omer*: the ritual counting of each of the 49 days between the holidays of Passover and Shavuot (Leviticus 23:15).

2 *But the earth abideth forever*: Ecclesiastes 1:4 ("One generation passeth away, and another generation cometh: but the earth abideth for ever").

Chapter 3

3 *Tefillin*: also known as phylacteries. These are boxes filled with scriptural passages that observant Jewish men attach to their foreheads and arms during morning prayers. There was a difference of opinion between the famous rabbi and commentator Rashi and his grandson, known as Rabbeinu Tam, as to the order of the Biblical verses found in the phylactery boxes. Rashi's opinion was almost universally adopted, but sometimes the order of Rabbeinu Tam's was used as a sign of distinct piety.

4 *Aliye* (plural, *aliyes*): the honor of reciting the blessings before and after one of the sections of the Torah portion read weekly on the Sabbath in the synagogue.

Chapter 5

5 *God said to Jacob, 'Fear thou not, O my servant Jacob*: phrase from the beginning of a liturgical poem for the end of the Sabbath; this line quotes from Jeremiah 46:27–28:

> But fear not thou, O my servant Jacob, and be not
> dismayed, O Israel: for, behold, I will save thee
> *God said to Jacob, 'Fear thou not, O my servant Jacob*:
> phrase from the beginning of a liturgical poem

> Fear thou not, O Jacob my servant, saith the Lord:
> for I am with thee; for I will make a full end of all
> the nations whither I have driven thee: but I will not
> make a full end of thee, but correct thee in measure;
> yet will I not leave thee wholly unpunished.

6   *Mikveh*: a Jewish ritual bath.

Chapter 6

7   *Tallis-bag*: the *tallis* is the ritual prayer shawl worn by men at morning services; it is customarily brought to and from the synagogue in a decorated bag.

8   *Hemdat Shlomo*: the title of three different works—including rabbinic responsa, sermons, and interpretations of the Talmud—by Shlomo Zalman Lipshits (1765–1839), chief rabbi of Warsaw. Lipshits himself became known by the title of his work. *Sefer ha-Yashar*: a very popular 13th-century ethical text.

Chapter 7

9   *Starosta*: (literally, "elder") a low-level local functionary, either official or traditional, responsible for various administrative duties.

10   *Michael to my right, Gabriel to my left*: A protective invocation to the archangels from the prayer *"Keri'at shema' 'al ha-mitah,"* which is recited before going to bed.

11   *the English disease*: rickets.

Chapter 8

12   *Magid of Kozhenits*: Israel ben Shabetai of Kozenits (c. 1737–1814), a Rabbinic scholar and important early Hasidic figure in central Poland.

Chapter 10

13   *Elul*: Jewish month, from mid-August to mid-September, traditionally a time of soul-searching and repentance in the run-up to the High Holidays.

14   *Oh, Man . . . His origin is dust and his end is dust . . .* : A line
     from the prayer "*U-netaneh tokef*" from the High Holiday
     liturgy. At this point in the novel it is Elul, the month imme-
     diately preceding the High Holidays.

15   *Oh, do not cast me away in my old age . . .* : Another line from
     the High Holiday liturgy.

Chapter 11

16   *Poultrywoman*: Lazar's cognomen, Kurnik, means "poultry-
     man." Fradl here is referred to as a *kurnitshke*—a woman
     poultryman—a play on both their trade and their name.

17   *kapores* (Heb. *Kaparot*): A traditional atonement ceremony
     performed the day before Yom Kippur. It typically involves
     the swinging of a live chicken or rooster or hen over the
     head of the penitent. The bird would subsequently either be
     slaughtered and the meat donated to the poor, or it would
     be sold and the proceeds handed out as alms.

Chapter 12

18   *Nakhes*: pleasure or pride, especially in someone else's ac-
     complishments, particularly those of a child.

19   *Titus's flea*: reference to a Talmudic story in which the impious
     and blasphemous Emperor Titus is punished by being tor-
     mented when a flea (or gnat) was sent up his nose to irritate
     his brain for seven years (Tractate Gittin 56b). The term has
     become synonymous with extreme irritation or vexation.

Chapter 14

20   *Under-tallis*: small ritual garment with fringes on each of its
     four corners, worn by men, usually under their shirts.

Chapter 15

21   *Then was our mouth filled with laughter, and our tongue with
     singing*: Psalm 126:2.

22   *Tailors' Synagogue*: In Eastern European Jewish communi-
     ties, professions often organized their own synagogues.

23 *Aliyes . . . Torah lifting*: The *aliye* (see earlier) is the honor of reciting the blessings before and after the weekly Torah portions on the Sabbath. During that part of the service, the honors (of lesser degree) include lifting the Torah to show to the community, and wrapping up the scroll.

24 *Ein keloheinu . . .* : lines from one of the final concluding songs of the Sabbath services.

Chapter 16

25 *Borukh she-omar*: the name of one of the introductory prayers of the Sabbath morning service.

26 *to hearken unto the tear-leaking and to the prayer*: This is a pun, based on I Kings 8:28: Hersh Lustik substitutes Yiddish *rinen* ("to leak") because it sounds like the Bible's Hebrew *rinah* ("a loud cry of supplication"). The text from I Kings reads: " . . . to hearken unto the cry and to the prayer, which thy servant prayeth before you today."

27 *Simeon and Levi*: a reference to Genesis 49:5–8, Jacob's deathbed curse of his sons, Simeon and Levi, for their great anger.

28 *Because of the shaft of a litter, Betar was destroyed*: reference to a Talmudic story describing the cause of the destruction of the fortress of Betar during the Bar Kochba revolt. The custom was for a tree to be planted on the birth of a child: a cedar for a boy and an acacia for a girl. When the child was eventually married, branches of those trees would be used for his or her wedding canopy. It happened that the daughter of the Roman emperor was traveling through the region and the shaft of her litter broke. Soldiers cut off branches of one of these cedars to repair it. The Jews attacked the soldiers, and word was sent to Rome that the Jews were in revolt, instigating the suppression (see Tractate Gittin 57a).

29 *even though Israel sinned*: Talmud, Tractate Sanhedrin 44a.

30 *Aleinu*: the concluding prayer of the Sabbath morning service.

Chapter 17

31 *Berek Joselewicz*: Berek Joselewicz (1764–1809) was an officer

in the Polish army, famous for having formed the first all-Jewish military unit, under Tadeusz Kościuszko.

32 *Money oppresseth all*: see Ecclesiastes 10:19. Hersh here makes a subtle pun on the biblical verse. The Hebrew text reads: "Money answereth all things." The same verb, vocalized slightly differently, has the meaning Hersh gives it: "Money oppresseth all (people)."

33 *From Błonie*: An idiomatic reference to a vengeful person. Błonie is also the town, near Warsaw, where Bursztyn was born.

Chapter 18

34 *Dunam*: an Ottoman unit of land measurement of roughly 90 square meters. Twenty *dunams* is something under half of an acre.

35 *Reduced to a loaf of bread*: compare Proverbs 6:26—"For by means of a whorish woman a man is brought to a piece of bread."

36 *As a father pitieth his children*: Psalm 103:13—"As a father pitieth his children, so the Lord pitieth them that fear Him."

37 *Your eye shall not look with pity*: Genesis 45:20—"And your eye shall not look with pity upon your things, for the good of all the land of Egypt is yours."

38 *none did compel*: Esther 1:8—"And the drinking was according to the law; none did compel: for so the king had appointed all the officers of his house, that they should do according to every man's pleasure."

Chapter 19

39 *But challah, bosor ve-dogim shall you eat every Sabbat*: a paraphrase of a line from a Sabbath hymn: *bosor ve-dogim ve-khol mat'amim*—"meat and fish and all tasty things."

Chapter 20

40 *Danzig*: After the First World War, Danzig (Gdańsk) had been designated a "Free City" under the Treaty of Versailles and became a bone of contention between Germany and

Poland. The Nazis took control of the city in the early 1930s and repatriation of the city became a major objective of the Party. Eventually, returning Danzig to Germany would be one of the pretexts for the invasion of Poland in 1939.

Chapter 21

41 *God of Abraham*: A Yiddish prayer recited by women at the conclusion of the Sabbath.

42 *Va-yiten lekho* . . . : The Hebrew phrases come from the first line (excerpted from Genesis) of the hymn following the Havdalah service on Saturday evening, concluding the Sabbath. Hersh alternates the italicized Hebrew phrases with satirical rhyming Yiddish. (Genesis 27:28—"Therefore *God give thee* of the dew of heaven, and *the fatness of the earth, and plenty of corn* and wine.")

43 *Maharal*: Rabbi Yehudah Leib ben Betsalel of Prague (d. 1609), known as the Maharal, was a famous religious scholar, philosopher, and mystic.

Chapter 22

44 *Punim*: Polish Yiddish pronunciation of *ponim*, "face."

45 *Only one son*: The Yiddish idiom for an only son is *an oyg in kop*, literally "an eye in the head." The poignancy of the usage here is underscored by the repeatedly emphasized fact of Khashe having only one good eye.

Chapter 25

46 *Bney Heykholo*: a Hasidic hymn, often sung during the third Sabbath meal.

47 *You shall not look with pity* . . . : Compare *inter alia* Genesis 45:20 and Isaiah 13:18.

Chapter 26

48 *Bal-Bris*: the father of a child to be circumcised.

49 *Hanukkah* . . . *Lag b'Omer*: Hanukkah starts on the 25th of *Kislev* (in December). Lag b'Omer is the 18th of *Iyar* (in April

or May). There are 141 days between them, far too few for a typical pregnancy.

50 *A packet of Psalms*: among the folk rituals surrounding a woman in labor, copies of Psalm 121 would be put around her room, intended both to ease labor as well as to protect mother and newborn.

Chapter 27

51 *Aliyes*: As mentioned earlier, when the Torah is read during Sabbath services, the passage is divided up into seven portions. At the beginning of each portion a different member of the congregation is called up to recite a benediction before and after the reading of that portion. Being given an *aliye* is considered a special honor. Traditionally, the first two *aliyes* are given to a *Kohen* and a *Levi*—descendants of the priestly and Levitical families, respectively. The final portion, called the *maftir*, is given to the person who would recite the *haftarah*, the assigned reading from the Prophets following the Torah reading.

52 *Mizrahist*: *Mizrahism* refers to a religious Zionist political organization in Poland in the first third of the 20th century.

53 *Osman Pasha*: Osman Pasha (1832–1900) was an Ottoman field marshal. He was famously defeated at the Siege of Pleven (Bulgaria, 1877) during the Russo-Ottoman war of 1877–1888. Despite his surrender, he was regarded as a hero.

54 *Nishmas*: One of the last introductory prayers during the morning service on Sabbaths and holidays.

55 *Va-yiloynu ho-om*: Genesis 15:24—"And the people murmured [against Moses]."

56 *switching the "who hath chosen" with the "who hath given"*: During an *aliye*, prayers are recited before and after the reading of each of the individual Torah passages. The prayers share some similarities.

Before the reading: "Blessed art Thou, oh Lord our God, king of the universe, who hath chosen us [*bokhar bonu*] from among all the nations and hath given us the Torah."

After the reading: "Blessed art Thou, oh Lord our God, king of the universe, who hath given us [*nosan lonu*] the Torah of truth, and planted eternal life within us. Blessed art Thou, oh Lord, who giveth the Torah."

57 *Panie Komisarzu*: Polish, "Mr. Police Commissioner."

Chapter 28

58 *tzitzis-fringe*: the knotted fringes worn on the corners of the *tallis* (prayer shawl) and under-*tallis* (a ritual garment worn by men under their shirts).

59 *What profit hath a man of all his labor? . . . vanity of vanities*: from Ecclesiastes 1:2–3.

Chapter 29

60 *Hotzenplotz* (Polish, *Osobłoga*; Czech, *Osoblaha*): German name for a town in Silesia, in present-day Czech Republic. It became a metonym in Yiddish for some place remote.

61 *ramakh eyvrim . . .* : The body is traditionally believed to contain 248 organs and 365 sinews, which total 613, the number of commandments Jews derive from the Torah.

Chapter 30

62 *. . . to immerse himself in the mikveh in the morning . . .* : Jewish law requires purifying immersion in a *mikveh*, a ritual bath, for any number of reasons, including when a man has a nocturnal emission.

Chapter 31

63 *Out of the mouth of babes and sucklings*: Psalm 8:3—"Out of the moth of babes and sucklings has thou ordained strength because of thine enemies, that thou mightiest still the enemy and the avenger."

64 *The Lord hath chastened me sore*: Psalm 118:18—"The Lord hath chastened me sore: but he hath not given me over unto death."

65 *lulav*: a bundle of palm, myrtle, and willow branches carried and ritually shaken on the festival of Sukkot.

66   *Let us search our ways*: Lamentations 3:40.

67   *His breath goeth forth*: Psalm 146:4.

Chapter 33

68   *Kol zman she-haneshomo be-kirbi*: "For as long as my soul is within me"—A phrase from one of the prayers recited every morning upon rising.

Chapter 34

69   *And Joseph died ... Now there arose a new king*:

> *And Joseph died*, and all his brethren, and all that generation.
> And the children of Israel were fruitful, and increased abundantly, and multiplied, and waxed exceedingly mighty; and the land was filled with them. [...]
> *Now there arose a new king* over Egypt, which knew not Joseph. (Exodus 1: 6, 8)

A reference to the death of Jósef Piłsudski (1867–1935), military and political leader of Poland, first head of state of Poland's Second Republic, after the First World War, and one of the founders of the modern state. Piłsudski was considered by many the lesser of evils for Polish Jewry. After his death in 1935, the Jewish situation in Poland deteriorated.

70   *Bratslaver*: Nahman of Bratslav (1772–1811), the founder of a popular and charismatic Hasidic movement in the early 19th century.

Chapter 36

71   *Ophir*: an Eastern land mentioned in various places in the Bible, notably from which Solomon received gold, precious stones, and other luxury goods.

Chapter 37

72 *Hay-vay, ta-ta-lo, ta-ta-lo!*: the Yiddish would be: *"Ay vay, tatele, tatele!"*—"Woe is me, my dear papa!"

73 *Yis-ga-dal ve-yis-ka-dash*: the first words of the Kaddish, a mourning prayer.